The Fundamentalists

Inside the Group

By D. A. Alan

The Fundamentalists

This is a work of fiction. Names, characters, places and events are from the author's imagination. Other than known historical people specifically named or globally recognized writings specifically named in the book, any resemblance of people living or dead, places, or events are entirely coincidental.

This book does not provide any quotes, specific commentary, or opinions on books referenced within this writing. The books are only refenced as props the characters would naturally use as a reference.

Any ideas or statements referenced from historical figures in this book are not intended to be actual quotes or the figure's actual intent. The figures are only mentioned in the book in context of how the characters see them.

Published by D. A. Alan
daalanseeking@gmail.com

Foreword

I have found it very difficult to explain to my children my childhood. Thankfully the idea of growing up in a cult is something they cannot grasp. I wrote this book to give them a sense of what it is like to live in an environment isolated and closed off from the surrounding world.

My intent is not to call out any polygamy group in particular. The book is fictional. All characters and locations come from my imagination. That being said, the challenges the characters face and the experiences they have are reflections of my life growing up in polygamy.

I had a very fun childhood full of adventures with my cousins. We lived on a property where it was just us, and we made the best of it. It was not until I was in my teenage years before I started feeling and seeing the damaging lifestyle I was raised in.

I do not see fundamentalist people as bad or ignorant. Most of them are some of the most caring people you would ever meet. The problem lies in their beliefs. Once I made it to my thirties, I had a falling away that finally exposed my groomed mind to the backwards and toxic effects a polygamous lifestyle can have.

Growing up this way, the environment feels normal and at home. My identity was completely wrapped up in the culture, so much that leaving was like shredding who I was. Years away and life on the outside still does not feel fully normal.

There is a chapter in the book titled, "Complexity." This is an important concept for me. We are so quick to judge people for their beliefs. One thing I have learned is everyone has a background. Their experiences build their lives into the complex and wonderful human they are. If there is one thing to take away from this book it would be to be more understanding of people, no matter who they are. You never know what someone was exposed to in life or what pains they have endured.

My efforts in this book are to show my depiction of life in polygamy, the good, the bad, and the ugly. There are many stories I know from people that come from my background. Mine is a mild tale. I will leave it up to others to share their stories if they so choose.

Part I

The Group

Chapter 1
The Group

They call themselves the Group. A remnant of a bygone era, the Group strives to keep alive the doctrines and beliefs of American religious icons Joseph Smith and Brigham Young.

Cast off and rejected by the mainstream church established by Joseph Smith, the Group claims the Church has gone astray and lost all powers and rights given from God. Being the worthy heir, the Group claims to be the one and only true caretakers of these beliefs and are the only organization on Earth fully recognized and sanctioned by God.

All members of the Group believe they are still true and worthy members of the Church founded by Joseph Smith. The Church, they call the Mother Church, has brushed them aside and aggressively persecuted them. They were thrown out of the house because they held to the founding principles. Holding true, they see themselves as the Father Priesthood. The father has the responsibility to keep the house secure. Kicked to the curb, but one day the Father and Mother will be reunited as God intended.

The Group has a legal name. On paper their name is the Apostles United for God. This name is only to satisfy the legal demands of being an organization. No members think of themselves as the Apostles United for God or AUG. Not wanting to be called out by the Church, the members have unceremoniously adopted the name the Group.

The foundation for the Group's beliefs rests in the late 1800s, where, in their eyes, the Church caved to the world and apostatized from their founder's teachings. God, in His infinite wisdom, found a way to keep Joseph Smith's vision alive. The start of the Group can be traced to September 1886 where the Church leaders came together in a secret eight-hour meeting.

The legends of this meeting rival those of mythical Gods, whose powers were discussed through the ages. Such things occurred like Jesus manifesting himself to members and Joseph smith visiting from beyond the grave. There was light beyond all brightness, and even members levitating above the ground.

Power and glory abounded in this eight-hour meeting. It was a meeting you would expect God would construct if the entireness of eternity hung in the balance.

The conclusion from the meeting was a select group of men were set aside for one purpose, keeping alive Joseph Smith's vision, which was Celestial Plural Marriage, or as the world sees it, polygamy. The Group, needing a believable pathway, claims all authority from this meeting.

From the eight-hour meeting the power and authority endowed from God is now held by the leaders of the Group. The code name they use for these powers is the keys, meaning the keys needed to get one into the Celestial Kingdom.

These keys are so important that among the grand level of beings, the Group is on top. All of humanity will ultimately need to pass through the Group if they too want to get to the Celestial Kingdom. Their leader, Levi

Jacobs, is literally God's mouthpiece on earth. Holding these precious keys, how could he not be?

The Group has many beliefs, too many to dictate here, but a summary of their foundational beliefs will paint the picture of what it means to be a member of the Group.

To them, the highest and most important of these beliefs rest in what they call the fullness of the Gospel. The pinnacle of all beliefs is Celestial plural marriage and the United Order. These beliefs are so pivotal that the act of executing them alone does not suffice. Practicing these beliefs is only allowed if sanctioned by God.

For the Group, this means a person must be endowed. Without an endowment, God is not able to assess one's worthiness.

Being endowed is to be given the secrets to enter heaven. These secrets are so sacred that to know them, one must make covenants of Obedience, Chastity, Sacrifice, Consecration, and the Law of the Gospel.

The secrets are administered through special handshakes and movements of the arms along with secret names. If one does not have these, God will see their unworthiness and will not let the person into the Celestial Kingdom.

The endowment is given in temples. Since the Church has control of the temples, the Group has established endowment houses, which are lesser than a temple but are cleansed so that they can still be used for giving the endowment.

One must never speak of what goes on inside the endowment house. These things are so sacred, that penalty oaths are accompanied with the covenants to ensure members never reveal their sacred secrets.

Group members getting the endowment are not allowed to learn anything about the endowment prior to participating in the ceremony. They literally learn on the job so to speak. Flying blind, members of the Group make decisions that affect their whole eternity.

Heaven to a member of the Group is not abstract. Heaven is very well defined. The Structure is as follows:

Highest Order of Celestial Kingdom: only reserved for those with many wives.

Celestial Kingdom: God resides here. This place is reserved only for endowed people. Endowed men and wives will be able to have children. Others not endowed may reside here but will not be able to have children. They will be servants to the endowed. These would be the Mother Terresa's of the world.

Terrestrial Kingdom: This is a lower kingdom reserved for those who were good people but were not endowed.

Telestial Kingdom: Sinners, murderers, people of lower caliber.

Outer darkness: Those members of the Group who were endowed and apostatized, rejecting the endowment covenants.

The symbol all Group members wear to demonstrate they are endowed is special under clothing called garments. The garment is worn for the rest of their lives. Once placed on a person, they must never remove them for more than twenty-four hours at a time.

Regarding clothing styles, you may be thinking of odd hair and prairie dresses, but that is not that case with the Group. The members can easily blend into a crowd. At first glance, they do not look out of the ordinary. To find a member of the Group, scan a crowd on a hot summer's day. Seek for the person looking very uncomfortable in unnecessarily long clothing. Nine times out of ten this person will be a member of the Group.

Why do they wear long clothing you might ask? The garments are a protection to the Group. Sleeves to the wrists and pants to the ankle, the full body needs protection. Hence long clothes are needed to hide this symbol of holiness.

The endowment, along with plural marriage, unlocks the grand achievement of the Celestial Kingdom; men can become Gods themselves. As Gods the celestial beings create billions of offspring to populate a new planet of their own. This is the plan of the Gods. Everything the Group does is with this one purpose, the path to Godhood.

The next brushstroke to understanding the Group is to switch directions on eternity and look backwards in time. The railroad of eternity does not start at birth. Life on this planet is a very brief pit stop in eternity. This life is like picking up all the needed fuel for the train to reach its destination. The stop is short, but without it the train would rust to nothingness, never moving the locomotive forward.

Looking backwards on this railway we see ourselves as pre-mortal children of Gods who were once as we are now. Your next question might be, "Why do we not remember this past life?" Well, God, in his infinite wisdom, chose for us to have no recollection of this pre-life as it would skew our ability to experience this current life to its fullest.

The idea of pre-existence has mind bending implications. If there truly is a pre-life existence, its impact would surely connect into our current life. For the Group, that is exactly the case. Our pre-mortal decisions thread through our sub-conscious, molding who we are in our present earthly form.

The Group believes that we had a choice to come to this earth. There was a great war in heaven. Satan led the rebellious. Those on Satan's side became beings without bodies that were cast down to earth to torment and test us. Ghosts, to the Group, are these unholy devils.

The most valiant children fought with Jesus and came down to this earth with bodies of flesh and blood.

What about those who didn't choose sides? The Group has an answer for this as well. Those who fought for Jesus can be seen here on earth with white skin. Those people who would not choose a side were, you may have guessed it, cursed with a skin of darkness.

God, in his love, still allowed these fence sitters to come down to earth but there had to be a price. God, in his infinite wisdom, chose to take this knowledge away so the person would never know of this rebellion.

Focusing too much on these eternal beliefs will distract from the tale at hand, but suffice it to say, almost all the filth spewing from the Group comes from these pre-mortal and post-mortal beliefs.

These eternal beliefs take otherwise good and decent people and churn them into the poison apple of society. To understand these two beliefs is to understand in large part who the Group is at its core.

....

The next facet to understanding the group is understanding how they see themselves in relation to God. The Group believes they are given power from God in a patriarchal wizardry they call the Priesthood.

There are two levels of Priesthood in the Group. The lower level is called the Aaronic Priesthood. This level of Priesthood gives no effectual power to the individual. It is more of a preparatory Priesthood for the Greater Priesthood called the Melchizedek Priesthood.

The Aaronic Priesthood is typically reserved for boys. When a boy comes of age to around eighteen, he is given the Melchizedek Priesthood.

The Melchizedek Priesthood is not just a symbolic title. The Group believes a person holding this Priesthood is given special powers from God. Depending on their level of faith, the powers of the Melchizedek Priesthood arm a man with abilities to withstand all attacks from an adversary.

The powers of the Priesthood are as follows: Cast out evil spirits, heal the sick using consecrated oil as a medium, speak in tongues, obtain revelation from God in personal and family matters, provide direction and guidance to individuals as a medium for God. Predict the future course of a child at birth, predict the future course of individuals as they come of age through a Patriarchal blessing, see the face of God and not burn, call down angels from heaven, and most importantly, not go crazy due to the demands of being married to several women at once.

The Priesthood, in essence, turns men into wizards for God. They are on the front lines, ready for whatever the devil might throw their way.

As is probably clear by now, the Group is a patriarchal society. So where do women fit in all of this? Women play the role of helpmeet to the men, as Eve was a helpmeet to Adam.

A woman's crowning achievement in life is bearing children. As all humanity existed prior to this life and are waiting to come down to this world to receive bodies, the more children a woman can have the better. Each child born into the Group is brought into the holiest part of the Earth. If the women did not have these children, the pre-mortal entities would be doomed to be raised in the world by gentiles.

....

As the painting continues to texture the canvas, the structure of the Group is the next important element.

The Group is led by a Council. The official title of the Council is "the Council of Friends". The Group refers to them as the Council for short. The Council is led by one man who is God's mouthpiece on earth. He is thought to be a true and living prophet whom God uses to dictate edicts for all of humanity.

The council controls all activities in the Group by organizing them in collective social structures. The social structure of the Group lies within the second law of the fullness of the Gospel. This second law is called the United Order.

The Group aspires for Zion. To them Zion is a place where God will reign for a thousand years. All people will work together for the good of the whole.

A United Order is a Zion in preparation so to speak. One sacrifices everything they have, or in other words, consecrates everything they have to God. Families then form a community pod where they strive to have all things in common. Each community in the Group is an established United Order. Each Order is led by a bishop who is appointed by the Council.

Not All Endowed men are part of the United Order. To become a member of a United Order, the Order must vote to let a man and his family in. Once in, the men covenant with each other to give all they have for the good of the whole.

The United Orders typically start with a joint effort to buy a piece of land. All members agree to purchase the land and then each is deeded a portion.

The land deeds are only valid so long as the man is a part of the order. If the man chooses to leave a United Order, he leaves with no compensation. In turn, the United Order helps fund the man to build his home and grow his business.

Now all of this is in theory of course. The utopian concept of Zion relies on complete selflessness of individuals. As this is rarely a human trait, conflicts and tensions arise as some are more successful and others are more motivated to live off the backs of others rather than to contribute their fair share. United Orders, in fact, have a history of being complete and utter failures.

....

The final brush strokes to understanding the Group is to look at their view of God.

God, to the Group, was once a man on a planet like ours. His first-born son was Jesus. The Group sees the Godhead as God the father, Jesus Christ, and the Holy Ghost. All are separate beings with human form. The Holy Ghost can vary on who holds this role, but right now this role is filled by Joseph Smith.

Joseph Smith is they key thread for getting to God. The Group believes that every leader of the Group is tied. In other words, if you want to see Jesus, you must get approval from Joseph Smith. If you want to see Joseph Smith, you must get approval down the line of leaders until you get to the one living today, Levi Jacobs.

For this reason, following the current living prophet is paramount. If you lose this connection, you ultimately lose your connection to Jesus. This is the golden chain that keeps all members inline.

As will be shown in the story, these beliefs lead to actions taken by Group members that will seem unbelievable and strange to the ordinary person. Doubt if you want, but the Group continues forward.

This is the Picassoish portrait that is the Group. A curious footnote of Americana, their complexity is a Freudian envy of society. Our story lies deep within the oil stains of this canvas.

Chapter 2
Family

Speckled across the mountains of the Americas West are ten communities. Some of these communities are houses intermingled among towns and cities of the gentiles. Others are alone in sparsely inhabited deserts. A few are small communities on their own land bordering nearby gentile communities. A gentile community is any community not part of the Group.

These ten communities are the United Orders of the Group. One of the latter such Orders is at the base of a large and forested mountain range. Being over a thousand acres, the land provides enough separation from its surroundings that once entered, it feels like stepping into a whole new civilization. This plot of land is the Pleasant Hills United Order.

Spread across the acreage of Pleasant Hills, the United Order consists of several family groups. Ten different last names comprise the bulk of the Order. Being one of the larger United Orders, this community even houses three council members, Melvin Allen, Joseph Labaron, and Duane Widdle.

There are three nearby gentile communities. These are Greenfield, Jessop, and Hidden Valley. The nearest community, Greenfield, is about five miles from Pleasant Hills.

A recently paved road winds from Greenfield to Pleasant Hills. Slowly climbing the road towards Pleasant Hills, the landscape changes from green farmland into pine trees, with the entrance of Pleasant Hills being a quarter mile inside the pine trees.

Being over a thousand acres, the aptly named Pleasant Hills is full of rolling hills and deforested fields. The property is a very pretty corner of Earth. It even as two small streams running from the mountain side through the community.

The five-acre plot of land entering Pleasant Hills was deeded to Alma Thomas. Two women call Alma husband, his first wife Missy, and Jane. Complications from her last birth, Missy only had three children. From oldest to youngest, they are Ruth (13), Claire (11) and Nephi (10). Jane has five children, Alma (10), Lucy (8), Josiah (7), Marvie (5), and Lisa (2).

The family all lives under one roof. A polygamous house is a wonder in architecture. Designed to maximize space, the houses are two story boxes with some having an additional basement.

Polygamy houses are typically designed for future expansion. They are built large enough to accommodate the possibility of a future wife.

Being young when first married, Alma's house did not have a basement, causing the Thomas household to already be bursting at the seams with its residents.

The favorite wife, which all men have, ultimately will wiggle their way into the main part of the house with the next wife on the top level. When designed properly, A third wife will eventually move into an unfinished basement. A polygamous house will have a large family room in the center and a separate kitchen space for each wife.

In short, pick one house in Pleasant Hills and you have seen them all. As such, the Thomas residence was a variant of these architectural maximizers.

The Thomas family was a typical family in the Group. Children being raised almost entirely by overly stressed mothers, men spending most of their time away on United Order and Priesthood matters, the family served one purpose. That is raising the next generation of Group members.

Often fending for themselves the Thomas children were a close-knit group. They did everything together, most notably going on wild adventures into the forest. Even two-year-old Lisa played a role in these imaginative forays. Our story begins on the eve of one such adventure.

....

"Nephi, come on. Time for family prayer." Missy called through the hallway to her kids. Having done the routine since they were little, Ruth and Claire were up already. Even though the family does this pretty much every morning, all the other children could still not get their bodies to comply. "Let's go," Aunt Jane yelled from down the stairs. "Papa is needing to go to work."

A family that prays together is a family that stays together. This is a motto across the Group. The Thomas family ritualistically said family prayers together before Alma headed off to work. This was an absolute requirement for him. Rain or shine, healthy or sick, morning family prayers were never missed. There were no exceptions, well, unless Alma was away for a business trip. Then the mothers would have a little sympathy on the poor tired children.

Rubbing their eyes, all the children came out of their rooms. Together all facing northward, the family faced towards the main temple of the Church and knelt down. "He, He," Lisa started giggling. Being two years old, she was given liberties the other children were not privileged to have. Any noises from the other kids would be met with an immediate smack on the noggin by their father. Prayer was a serious matter.

Jane shushed Lisa. "Who do you want to pray this morning dear?" Jane asked. "I will say the prayer today," Alma replied. A mild groan was heard across the room. With Dad praying, the children all knew they would be on their knees for a long time. Alma was not amused. "Quiet now everyone. One more peep and you will spend the rest of the prayer in tears."

"Our Dear Heavenly Father," Alma began. After a pause, Alma started into his long pause-filled prayer.

All prayers in the Group follow a similar pattern. The amount of elaboration and depth depends on the person giving the prayer, but they are all basically the same. Dear Heavenly Father, bless loved ones, bless our day to be productive, no harm or accidents to befall us, no harm or accidents on the roads and highways (culturally slipped in over the years), bless Brother Levi and the Priesthood Council, bless the temple doors will be opened to the Group, thank you for everything you have provided, in the name of Jesus Christ, amen.

In a show of knowledge, reverence, and humble pride, priesthood men can take this template and drag it on for twenty minutes.

"Amen," Alma concluded. The younger children all being nudged awake, headed back to bed for another hour of sleep. Ruth and Claire headed to the kitchen.

The Thomas family was lucky that their first two kids were girls. Needing all the hands they could get, Ruth and Claire were cooking, cleaning, and taking care of their siblings since they were five.

As the kids woke up, they headed to the family table for breakfast. Ruth and Claire served their siblings while Missy and Jane prepared for school.

Adding one more element to the stress of a mother in the Group, mothers also hold the role of teacher as homeschooling is the preferred form of education. This is preferred as all elements of schooling can be done with intertwining education with Group beliefs. Reading is always scripture or a children's book on scripture. Math is counting bible men, and history is about the eight-hour meeting or stories of Church history.

For the Thomas family, three hours of school is all the mothers could handle before being totally drained.

Needing a daily breather, Jane and Missy would sweep the kids out of the house until the afternoon.

No thought was given to the kids during this break time. Pleasant Hills is large; everyone knows each other. Each day the Thomas kids were left to wander like a herd of lost sheep. Today was no exception. Schooling done; the Thomas kids headed on their next adventure.

....

"We are going into the forest," Claire said as the rag-tag Thomas kids headed up the hill. "Don't you think we should stop and pray?"

Ruth rolled her eyes. "We've got to hurry if we want to catch some coyotes." Ruth said. "Yeah com'on Claire," Nephi and Alma chimed in. "Not another step," Claire demanded, "until we kneel and pray for protection."

The children all knew that once set on something there was no stopping Claire. "Okay," Ruth said reluctantly, "let's all kneel." After a short silence, Ruth looked at Nephi. "You are the oldest boy. Who do you want to say the prayer?" Sheepishly not liking the situation he was in Nephi replied. "Claire this was all your idea. You say the prayer." "Don't mind if I do," Claire replied.

"Dear Heavenly Father," Claire started. "Wait," Alma jumped in. "What direction is the temple?" "Uh, I think it is that way." Ruth pointed northward. All the children turned in the same direction. "Can I begin now?" Claire glared at Alma.

"As I was saying," Claire continued. "Dear Heavenly Father, as we so jurn upon our mission, bless us that no harm nor accident will befall us or those on the roads and highways. Bless that when we find those mean coyotes Nephi and Alma won't run away scared like they often do. Bless that their guns will be pointed towards the coyotes and not Lisa. And bless that they will miss and only scare the coyotes."

"Claire," Nephi jumped in. "I want their hides." "Shush now," Claire hissed at Nephi. "You asked me to pray." Claire closed her eyes and continued. "Dear Heavenly Father bless that if the coyotes try to kill us your angels will come down and protect us. Also bless the temple doors will be open to us and bless Brother Levi and the council. In the name of Jesus Christ, Amen." "Amen," the clan all repeated. "A-a-a-m-e-n," Lisa echoed the call. The Thomas kids then headed up the hill in search of their prey.

After an hour without success, Alma and Nephi were deflated as they came back down the hill. They had no luck in the quest for a coyote hide. They didn't even see one. All they got was the chance to shoot their b-b guns at some birds in the trees.

The girls were in a jovial mood. Secretly they were glad no animals were harmed. Josiah, Marvie, and Lisa were just glad to be along and darted all over the hills. For them the adventure in the woods was worth the price of admission.

As they were coming down, Ruth picked up Lisa seeing she was starting to drag her feet. "I don't want to go all the way around to get to our house. Lisa is worn out." Ruth said. "Let's cut through the fields." "Next to brother Melvin's house?" Alma questioned, concerned with the path Ruth suggested. Alma continued, "No way, I'd rather walk around."

Ruth looked at the group. "My feet are killing me. Lisa is not going to make it." "No way, Alma's right." Nephi chimed in. Determined, Ruth headed towards the fence. "Suit yourselves," Ruth said and climbed over the wooden fence.

The remaining kids stood not sure what to do. Ruth was the oldest. Going back home without her was not something they wanted to attempt. Reluctantly the Thomas clan trailed after her.

Brother Melvin was an older man. One of three members of the council in the Order, he pulled a lot of sway in the community. As often happens as people age, children become less and less desirable to have around.

Brother Melvin had so many kids when he was younger that it warped his mind to the point that all kids today were a disease and were hell bent on causing him ilk. Other than his brother Reggie, it was not by chance that none of Melvin's family were part of the United Order. After his first wife passed away, the other wives either left him or just moved far away.

On most days the Thomas kids would have made it through unharmed, but today Melvin was out fighting old age in his garden and was in no good mood. The poor Thomas kids crossed the field and rounded the corner of Melvin's house right in front of him.

"Stop right there you little vermin!" Brother Melvin shouted. Adrenalin ran down the legs of the band of children as they took off in fright. The nemesis of every child, Nephi tripped over a loose shoelace and fell on his face.

"Help!" Nephi shouted, which brought the others to a halt. Turning around the children could see Brother Melvin in pursuit of the helpless Nephi. "I'll teach you for running in my fields." Melvin yelled. "Get up," Ruth shouted back to Nephi.

Seeing it was too late, Claire picked up a rock. Thwack, the pebble hit its mark right across Melvin's forehead. The velocity an eleven-year old can propel an object could not cause more than a bruise or a small goose bump. Seeing the reaction of Brother Melvin, you would think he was trampled by a wild bull. Brother Melvin fell on the ground writhing in pain. "I can't see. You nasty shits. My head. Owe. June do something." June was Melvin's late wife.

Seeing the opportunity Nephi got to his feet. The Thomas clan took off for home having successfully taken down their prey. This prey, however, the children knew was going to get them into a world of a mess.

The four oldest kids sat on the couch in the main living room. They could hear every word from what was happening outside. "Your kids attacked me. Look at the wound on my head. I will not stand for this." "Please

Brother Melvin, they will be punished." "Where is Alma?" "He is still at work." "Well woman you listen here. Those children have evil spirits raging through them. I swear I could see them frothing out of their mouths. The worst is that girl. What evil was running through her to smite a council member?" "Brother Melvin." "Don't you talk back to me. I am your priesthood head." "Now go and do your responsibility. You get control of those brats." Melvin turned and walked away.

Catching her breath, Aunt Jane came into the house. The four kids watched as she entered the living room. Anger was steaming from her forehead. Being brave and knowing he was the best shot to protect his sister, Alma spoke up. "She was protecting Nephi mom. You should have seen him." Jane cut him off. "Silence Alma. Claire, what do you have to say for yourself?" With her stubborn chin locked and loaded, Claire stood up.

"I did nothing wrong," Claire said defiantly. "What did you say?" Jane responded in disbelief. "I just saw the bruise on Brother Melvin's head. Now you get over here right now." Claire stood firm. "I did nothing wrong." This defiance sent the blood raging through Aunt Jane's system.

"Why you little," Aunt Jane stomped over to Claire. "I will teach you how to respect a council member." Claire knew what was coming but didn't care. She knew she had done the right thing and would take any consequence for it. Jane then let into Claire.

Missy had been grocery shopping when Melvin had stopped by. Hearing sounds from inside, Missy grabbed the bags of groceries and rushed into the house. Horrified, Missy dropped the groceries on the floor. "What are you doing?" Missy yelled. She had walked in a few minutes after Jane had started dishing out the punishment.

Missy ran over and pulled Jane away. "Get away from my daughter." Missy yelled. "You step back Missy." Jane replied. "You don't know what she has done." Jane was still in a fit of rage. Missy stepped into Jane's face. "I don't care. You have no right to punish my daughter." "Now leave!" She screamed as loud as she could.

Jane recoiled and stomped back away to her room. "We will be speaking to Alma about this." And she slammed her door. Missy picked up the sobbing Claire and took the poor girl into her room.

....

The challenges surrounding parenthood abound. Adding multiple parents and constant stress amplifies mistakes that parents make. Jane had gone too far, and she knew it.

After calming down, Jane found Claire with her mom in Missy's room. "Can I come in, Missy?" Jane asked. "Right now is not a good time." Missy replied angrily towards her sister wife. "I'm sorry." Jane said through the door and walked away.

Kids in large families have each other regardless of the number of adults in the household. Later that day the group stayed around Claire. Lisa and Marvie cuddled up to her not wanting anything else to happen. Jane could not bring herself to step outside her bedroom door. Seeing the kids all together sent her back in the room in tears.

Jane's punishment was not the end of the matter. Dad had not been informed yet. The kids all knew his punishment would be worse, and there would be no protection for Claire this time.

Nothing else was achieved that day. Both Missy and Jane stayed in their rooms. The kids, huddled around Claire, played games in the living room until dinner was needing to be prepared.

At this point the two mothers and Ruth gathered in the kitchen and began preparing the meal. No words were said, and preparations went on until Alma came home.

When dinner was ready, in fear the kids all sat down at the table. Alma looked around the table after blessing the food. Seeing the faces, Alma said, "Anything eventful happen today?" The kids dropped their heads. Missy began to speak, but Jane cut her off. "Nothing at all dear. The kids are just exhausted from a long day of playing in the field." "Oh," Alma said.

Turning to Jane and Missy, Alma continued. "You two let them play way too much. These faces say it all. I expect some more discipline in this house." Seeing his message had been received he put his head down and proceeded to eat.

Jane looked at Claire and mouthed, "I am sorry." Not ready to forgive but appreciating the cover up, Claire acknowledged Aunt Jane. The family proceeded with their meal.

Chapter 3
Community

Other than a few unconventional houses, driving into Pleasant Hills reveals nothing too out of the ordinary. The order consists of ten dominant families. That is to say, there are ten last names that make up the bulk of the Pleasant Hills Order. The main families are by last name, Allen, Thomas, Widdle, Jacobs, Partridge, Smith, Labaron, Bransen, Bailor, and Tannen.

The Group, like most isolated communities, have a lot of interrelated marriages. Marrying one's second cousin is very common. In some instances, first cousins are not off limits. All of this makes so that United Orders, and the Group as a whole, are like a community of one large extended family.

This leads to a closeness and familiarity amongst the members. The children easily make friends with one another as going to the neighbor's house is practically going to an aunt or uncle.

Interactions with the outside world are very infrequent. Although Greenfield is just miles away, the propinquity is overshadowed by a wall of beliefs that keep the Group and the surrounding communities worlds apart.

The Group sees people in the world as sinners and, due to their rocky history of being persecuted, are feigned to openly trust anyone outside their close-knit circle. An outsider would be less than welcome when entering Pleasant   Hills. The Group have each other. That is the way they want it.

The combination of being isolated and closely related has a benefit of making a strong sense of community within the United Orders of the Group. The Pleasant Hills Order was no exception.

In the center of the community the Order poured a slab of concrete. The size is a little larger than the size of a tennis court. This slab, the Group called the Pad, was the focal point of all events in the Group. Sporting events, dances, games, community meals, general place of gathering, the Pad was the closest thing the Order had to a recreation center. On any given day one event or another was going on. Most commonly in the evening, the adult men were playing basketball.

....

Two years had passed since the altercation with brother Melvin. Jane's decision that night to protect Claire from Alma had softened what could have been a rift within the family. As such, the Thomas family had moved on from the event.

Life had gone on as normal for the most part until recently. For the past few weeks, frequent arguments were had amongst the parents. Tension filled the halls of the Thomas residence.

The pot started boiling over this weekend, which started off as innocent as any other. The community was gathered at the Pad. The men and older boys were playing the ritual Saturday night basketball game.

Alma Thomas was in his element when playing sports. Alma loved playing with the younger men and teenage boys. The Thomas kids loved watching their dad play. He was a different person in a competitive arena. Winks to his girls, high fives to his boys, these were the interactions Alma had with his children that made them love him.

"Go Dad," Nephi yelled as Alma scored a bucket. The whole community had come out tonight. This game had drawn all the men of the Order, and it was quite the game. The hill around the Pad was packed with the whole Order.

"Not this time." Benji Jacobs yelled at Nephi as he taunted the Thomas family after stealing the ball from Alma and scoring on the other side. "I hate Ben," young Alma spouted. Being eighteen, Ben was able to run circles around the older guys. And he loved it. Ben was also the community bully. If there wasn't a kid to tease, Ben did not know what to do with himself.

"Shut up Ben," his best friend Willie Allen playfully elbowed his friend. Willie was two months younger than Ben. The two were best friends. Willie was a pressure relief for the pair. Where Ben was there to tease, Willie was there to pull him back just enough to give the kids a break.

The older girls were all sitting together. "You tell him Willie," Sallie Johnson yelled. Ruth cheered in agreement. Being fifteen, Ruth was just barely old enough to be allowed to sit with the older crowd. She was three years younger than Sallie.

"Y'all leave my Benji alone," Wendy Bransen chided the girls. She had picked Ben to be hers since they were small and always defended him. All the girls laughed. "Ooh Wendy, you gonna go kiss your beau," Ruth teased. Being the young one, this was unacceptable.

"You listen here youngster," Wendy was ready to go at poor Ruth, who was just trying to join in the fun. Sallie jumped in quickly. "Enough Y'all let's watch the game, and Benji too." Sallie smiled as she teased her friend and then turned and gave Ruth a wink.

The game had come to an end. Alma came over and chatted up with his boys and gave Ruth a hug. "I'm heading home, don't stay up too late." Alma said. "Don't you want to hug Claire?" Ruth asked. "Where is she?" Alma replied. Ruth looked around but didn't see her. "Is that girl off on another adventure?" Alma asked. Ruth nodded her head. "I've got to get going," Alma said. With that Alma was off heading back home with Missy and Jane.

For the kids of the Pleasant Hills United Order, the Saturday basketball game was only the start of the evening. They all waited in anticipation for the game to end. After that, the kids stayed for night games.

Claire was one of the few kids that did not get too into these sporting events. Outside her own family she did not get along too well with most of the other kids. Whenever the Group would get together Claire would inevitably go off on her own. She was not disliked by anyone. She participated and played with the other kids, but she was always an outsider and never bonded with any of the kids her age.

"Come on Claire." Ruth yelled when she finally found Claire out by the cars. "Night games are about to begin." Night games were the party scene of the Order kids. The kids from eighteen down to five congregated at the Pad every weekend. They would play every team game they could think of and were quite imaginative in creating their own games.

The game this night was Red Rover. The kids paired off on opposite ends of the Pad, and the game began. One by one the kids called each other over. "Red Rover Red Rover send Margie right over."

Little Margaret Widdle finally had her chance. Off she went with all determination right into the arms of the other kids. Margie did not pick her spot well and was quickly on her back after running right into the arms of two older boys.

All the kids laughed with glee. Their aim was not at Margaret, just at the success of defending their stone wall. Little Margie was heartbroken at her failed attempt and took off to the corner crying.

"Poor thing," Sallie thought to herself and was about to console Margie. Before she had a chance, Claire had broken away and was at Margie's side giving her comfort.

This left a mark on Sallie as none of the other kids had any consideration for what had happened. Sallie went over and gave the two girls a hug and rubbed Claire's head. "You are so sweet," she said to Claire. Claire responded with a smile and took Margie back to the game.

Inevitably the time had finally arrived for the games to come to an end. Shouts from the distance could be heard from mothers calling for their children. The only problem was after night games came the time all children feared more than anything, heading home in the dark.

Being on the edge of the property, the Thomas residence was one of the more arduous journeys home. The Thomas clan gathered around, preparing for the sprint to safety.

Not long into the journey, perils began to arise. "Did you hear that?" Josiah said. "You all are so silly." Ruth replied, trying to be the brave older sibling. "There's nothing to worry about." She was convincing to no one. Having no other choice, the foursome continued into the unknown.

Not too much further into their journey the children heard the sum of all their fears. In the trees they heard the sound of coyotes and cougars.

"We're going to get eaten," Alma screamed; the clan took off in a sprint. Not daring to see their backside, the children ran at lightning speed until finally they were safe and sound at the footsteps of their home. Willie and Ben were in the trees rolling with laughter.

....

Religion is a twenty-four seven endeavor for the Group, but there is a day among days. This day is where sweat does not come from exercise, no, sweat comes from tightly fitting professional costumes designed for God's catwalk. Work stops on this day. Shopping has lost its appeal. Sports are forgotten. This day is Sunday.

For six days God did work and on the seventh he rested. Somewhere the count got mixed up, but God knows Sunday is now his day. Disrespect this day, and eternal consequences are on the line. This is a day of rest. Well, rest from labors that is. Because, for the Group, Sundays are anything but restful.

Time slows down on Sunday. For the Group, God has decreed endless meetings talking about how awesome God is and how pitiful and faulty we are as fallen beings.

For men, the day starts at five in the morning. An hour drive later and a two-hour Priesthood meeting is held at the Group Headquarters in Scottsdale. An hour drive back home and Sunday school is about to start. The family joins the party at this point and stays together for the rest of the day.

Being short for a meeting, Sunday school is an hour and a half. A quick lunch and then the family are loaded into the car for another hour trip to Scottsdale where a two-hour sacrament meeting is held in a building designed for boredom.

The Fundamentalists

Sacrament meeting is a hodgepodge of speakers taking turns with off-the-cuff sermons spoken in the dullest monotone language imaginable.

Prior to the speeches, forty-five minutes are spent in absolute silence renewing the baptismal covenants by taking a sacrament of bread and water. This water is so special that all members must drink from the same blessed cup.

Once this pinnacle of meetings ends, another hour-long drive home embarks. Finally, it is time for an evening fireside designed to one last time stroke God's ego.

Somewhere between all this the women cook the most elaborate meal of the week. The one nice thing for the kids on Sundays is they get to sleep in. Dad, in his mercy, gets up so early that even he has pity not to wake the kids. As night games almost always occur Saturday nights, this added rest is a much-needed reprieve before the long drawn out Sunday.

....

Jane loved the children, but to her, children needed firmness and strict rules. She was of the sort that any slip in the kid's behavior needed immediate correction. A lot of this is how she was raised. Love and affection were an afterthought in the Jacobs family.

Missy, on the other hand, was the gentle loving mother to all the kids, probably caring less about their development than she should.

Together, the two made a good parenting pair. They were a good balance of discipline and affection. After years together they had formed a symbiotic sisterhood, taking cues from each other in raising the children. This relationship had been working well up until recently.

The Thomas kids were extra tired on this particular Sunday. The longer than normal night games and chase from the cougars the prior night had done them in.

One by one they came down to breakfast prepared by Ruth and Claire. "Hurry up kids, everyone to their place at the table." said Aunt Jane, the enforcer of the sister wife team. She was to see to it that the kids grew up to be the most holy and righteous Thomas representatives possible. "No more lingering around. We got to eat so we can start family scripture study." Jane said.

"Ooh," a collective gasp was heard around the table. "Jane, let's give the kids a break," Missy said looking at the sleepy eyes. "Missy, the kids need to study." Jane gave a look of displeasure at her sister wife. Missy threw her hands up. "They're all yours." She said in anger and went to her room. Jane, not liking Missy's reaction, followed suit and threw her apron on the floor and stomped off. The kids sat staring at each other.

"What is wrong with momma?" Josiah asked, to no one in particular. These types of outbursts had become common in the last few weeks. Ruth and Claire were taking the brunt of these skirmishes as it left the work to them.

Ruth looked over at Claire. "At it again," she said with a roll of her eyes. "Alma, Nephi, take the kids into the living room." Claire said. "Lucy, come help clean up." The older kids began making preparations for the day.

Claire and Ruth had completed the morning activities just in time for Sunday School. Once the children were ready, they waited for Alma to return from Priesthood meeting. Once he arrived, Missy and Jane exited their rooms and led the kids out the door.

Chapter 4
Chosen

The one meeting on Sundays designed for children was Sunday School. The Thomas kids enjoyed these meetings. Games, treats, and playing with friends were common in Sunday School meetings.

Ritualistic music highlights the beginning of the meeting where children hold signs to practice a new melody as a subconscious educator of the Group's beliefs. The children then break into separate meetings by age group. The parents stay behind where, in the eyes of the kids, their purpose is to establish a punishment chamber where naughty kids go when they act up during their lessons.

The Bishop, Brother Korban Bransen, was teaching the thirteen-year old class on this Sunday. His lesson was on the elevated level the Group had been placed upon the Earth.

"Kids, did you know you had the opportunity to choose your family before you came to this earth?" Bishop Bransen began. Brother Bransen chose pre-mortal existence as the best scenery to make his point. "You were the more most righteous of God's children in heaven. For your righteousness, you got to come down on earth to righteous parents, and you got to pick them."

"What about the less naughty kids in heaven?" Billy Widdle asked. Normally the kids at this age are unruly and not too interested in the lesson, but this topic had some intrigue. "That is a good question Billy." Brother Bransen replied.

"Are there poor kids in the world? Do you think they wanted to be in their situation?" The class looked at Brother Bransen not knowing the answer. Lorin Johnson raised her hand. "Is it because they sinned in heaven?"

"That is close," Brother Bransen replied. Billy was starting to get the message. "So, the more we achieved in heaven before we came here the more righteous families we get to come to?" Billy asked.

Still contemplating, Lorin chimed in again. "Does that mean if you were bad in heaven you get bad parents?" Bishop Bransen paused for a while contemplating the question. "Well I guess so in a way, yes." He responded.

Claire's mind was churning listening to this lesson. "Why would God punish kids to go to bad parents?" Claire asked inquisitively. This question caught Bishop Korban a little off guard. Now having to go off script and really think about what he was saying, Bishop Bransen responded. "God does not punish these kids. God is just. Because the people did not live up to their callings, God put them where they deserved to be."

Claire's mind was all over the place now. "Wouldn't God put kids that struggle in easier families. Wouldn't the stronger kids be given harder families?" Claire asked.

Starting to get a little frustrated, Bishop Bransen replied. "Claire, you were righteous in the pre-existence. You got to choose your parents. Claire, you tell me. Don't you think you are better than a boy born in Bangladesh?" Bishop Bransen put this back on Claire trying to show his point that kids in the Group were in a better situation than anyone else in the world.

"Where is that?" asked Katie Smith. "Asia," Brother Bransen replied and looked back at Claire. Claire pondered this for a while. "God loves all kids." She thought to herself. "I know God would love that kid." Claire then replied, "No i'm not. God loves all his children the same. He is no respecter of persons. Right?" "Well you are wrong Claire." Brother Bransen replied with a quip.

Changing his tone, Brother Bransen now spoke to Claire in a condescending manner. "You are better than that child. He did not reach your brightness in Heaven. Because of this, he didn't get to choose his life. You did. That is unless you would rather be in Bangladesh." Brother Korban made the last point mockingly at Claire.

All the kids picked up on the tone from Brother Bransen and started giggling at Claire's botched answer. Claire glared back, not liking being ridiculed.

....

After Sunday school the Thomas family were gathered around the family table for their Sunday lunchtime meal. Sunday lunch was a special meal. Not only was the food specially prepared, this was the one meal where the whole family could sit and talk.

Sunday meals were a family togetherness time. This was one of the few times father Alma was attentive to his kids and their questions. On Sunday their questions were mainly gospel related, so Alma was in his zone.

"Papa," Claire began, "Bishop Korban says we are more special than other kids. Is that true?" Alma replied, "yes you are dear. You are mine. That makes you special." Not liking the simple brushing off response, Claire continued. "Why does God not let other kids have families like ours?" "What do you mean?" Replied Alma.

Claire swallowed the lump in her throat. "Well, Bishop Korban says we got to choose our parents because we were better in heaven. Why can't other kids choose their parents? Wouldn't good parents be better for helping the kids in need?"

"You are silly Claire," Ruth spoke up. "It is in the scriptures." Ruth was referring to a book of teachings by Joseph Smith, which was canonized by the Group. This is where Brother Bransen had gotten his information.

Claire looked at her sister confused. Alma continued with a smile on his face. "Ruth is right dear. Jesus is our biggest brother. He was the best of all of us in the pre-existence. The next holiest were the prophets." "Like Brother Levi?" Nephi questioned. "Exactly." Alma replied. "Brother Levi was one of the holiest people in heaven. It all goes down from there. You can even see how holy people were in heaven by how they look and act on earth."

Not liking the racist direction the topic was turning and thinking Claire was on to something, Missy stepped in to steer the conversation back to the main question. "Claire has a point." Missy said. "I always struggle with why God puts kids in really bad situations."

Alma gave Missy a stern look. "Well she has a point Alma." Missy said after meeting his gaze. Not liking his continued gaze, Missy stood up. "Are you going to punish me for this as well?" She got up and walked away from the table.

Alma sat for a while staring in the same direction. After a moment, he got up and stomped into his office. Head down the entire conversation, Jane got up two minutes later and went to her room. Ruth and Claire were left once again to clean up the meal.

....

There was no time for discussion after lunch. The girls quickly cleaned the dishes. Knowing the drill, they got the kids into their fifteen-seat van, a vehicle that is a necessity among families in the Group.

Normally all the parents sat together in the front. Citing kid patrol, Missy sat in the back on this trip to sacrament meeting in Scottsdale. Other than Lisa, the Thomas family was not in a talkative mood and remained quiet the entire trip.

The headquarters of the Group sits in a bowl surrounded by mountain ranges. The compound consists of three buildings, the endowment house, a house used for office space, and a recreation building named after one of the Group's prior leaders. The Group just called the large building the REC for short. Spread out around the buildings are several houses where members of the Scottsdale Order resided.

The REC was an ingeniously designed building capable of housing the most fist to cuff basketball games on Saturdays and the most sacred of meetings the following Sunday.

The building was designed to maximize its usefulness. This made the building ill-suited for meetings. Being a gymnasium, the room echoes from end to end and has horrible air ventilation.

The Group were engineers at making their religious gatherings the most tortuous meeting experience possible. Every Sunday the REC would be filled to the brim with hard metal folding chairs. To continue the appeal to uncomfortableness, sacrament meetings are held in the afternoon and last for two hours.

The Group were masters of boredom. Long, hot, uncomfortable, sacrament meetings alone are a compliment for the dedication Group members have to their religion. No one would sit through such an awful experience if they did not truly believe the doctrine thrown their way.

All the Council members sit at the front of the meeting on a stage, clearly signifying their importance to everyone in the room. They also give most of the talks.

These talks are unrehearsed and off-the-cuff. In God's form of roulette, different Council members are selected to speak each week. Talented orators they are not. Nothing is less entertaining than old men mumbling about the most abstract concepts of the Gospel.

To ensure no pleasure is achieved, the Group starts all sacrament meetings with its namesake. Sacrament is passed through the congregation in a ritual that takes forty-five minutes, and no one is allowed to make a peep until sacrament is finished.

The smart people in the Group know how to navigate this meeting. The strategy for Sacrament meeting is seating. The earlier one can get into the REC the better. The standard is to get to the REC thirty minutes early. The seats on the side towards the back were the ideal placement. A family could sleep without getting noticed.

....

The Thomas family filed into their usual spot prior to Sacrament meeting starting. Alma and Jane were off making the rounds until it was time for the meeting to begin. Missy was in no mood on this Sunday to go and speak with extended family and friends.

As Alma and Jane returned, a woman was with them. The announcement was given that meeting was about to begin. Surprising the kids, the young woman came over with Alma and Jane. The woman sat next to Alma on the isle with Jane next to the kids.

"Who is that?" Nephi leaned over to Claire. "Why is she sitting by Dad?" "I don't know," Claire shrugged. Claire leaned over to her mom sitting next to her. "Mom, who is that next to Dad?" "Shush now." Missy said with an angry expression. "Meeting is about to begin."

Claire was a little surprised by her mother's expression, but she was not able to think long as Brother Duane Widdle got up to start the meeting. The whole congregation stood up, sang an opening song, were led in prayer, and then sat down.

The Sacrament bread and water was then passed through the congregation. An eternity of shushing children later, the sacrament was finished. The meeting then transitioned to the sermons.

Brother Widdle, leading the meeting today, leaned over to Brother Joseph Labaron. Brother Labaron struggled out of his chair and walked to the microphone.

Known for his 'glamorous' talks on Celestial Plural Marriage, Brother Labaron started into one of his favorite rants. "The fullness of the Gospel is the United Order and Celestial Plural Marriage." Brother Labaron scanned the audience and then began his fist pounding tirade. "Remember the eight-hour meeting brothers and sisters and the sacrifices to keep the principle alive."

Missy had heard this speech her entire life, but today it felt like this talk was directed at her. It almost seemed like Brother Labaron was speaking right to her. "You brethren, do not be satisfied with two. You must continue to grow your families." Brother Labaron said, clinching his fist.

Missy caught the glance from Alma. Missy's blood started boiling. Not able to stand the talk, she got up. "Mom, where are you going?" Claire whispered. "I am not feeling well. I need to get some air." Missy replied. "Can I come?" Claire asked. Missy paused for a second. "Sure dear," she replied and beckoned Claire to follow.

The two walked out the back of the building ignoring the stares from the congregation. Mother and daughter went and sat on the lawn by the side of the building. Not understanding what was going on Claire held her mother as she sat on the grass. Claire did not know what to say, and Missy was not eager to talk. The two just sat together until the meeting was over.

As the crowd left the REC, Claire found her family exiting out the back of the building. Alma saw Claire on the lawn and motioned over to her. Claire looked at her mom who had no desire to come along. Not sure what to do, Claire sat for a second. Missy gave her a little nudge letting her know it was okay to go. Claire then got up and went over to where the rest of the Thomas family had gathered.

"I want you all to meet someone." Alma said to the Thomas family surrounding him. He then pulled this new woman in front of him. "This is Pamila Smith." Alma said. Claire looked back at her mother and finally put the pieces together.

Alma introduced Pam, who nervously introduced herself to everyone. Claire kept her gaze on her mother who was covering her face with her hands. When it was Claire's turn to be introduced, she quickly exchanged introductions and went back to her mother.

The two sat again silently for a few more minutes before Nephi came over. "Mom, Claire, Dad says it's time to go." Nephi said. Looking his mom over for a moment, Nephi held out his arm to help Missy up. "Are you okay Mom?" Nephi asked. Missy nodded her head. "I'm okay son," she said. "Now help me up so we can go home."

As the three were walking to the van, Nephi leaned over to Claire. "It all makes sense now don't you think?" "Sure does." Claire nodded and glanced at her mother. "Seeing Dad with another woman is weird." Nephi said. "No more talking kids." Missy said overhearing the conversation. "Let's get to the van so we can get out of this place."

Chapter 5
Betrayal

Pamila Smith was from the Yuma Order, which was five hundred miles south of Pleasant Hills. She had ties to the Pleasant Hills Order as she was Jordan Smith's younger sister. Jordan had recently joined the order after moving from Yuma.

Pam had been in love with Alma since she was fifteen. Whenever she had the opportunity to come up north, she would always seek him out. Pam knew she was supposed to be married to Alma. In Pamila's mind, they knew each other in the pre-existence. Nothing was going to stop this fore-ordained union. Being eighteen now, she was ready to make her move.

Three months prior to the fateful Sunday meeting, Pam went to her father to let him know of her interest in Brother Thomas. After hearing the news, Pamila's father went through the channels to let Alma know his daughter was interested.

When Alma found out about Pamila's interest, he was very intrigued. This is the first girl that had ever expressed interest in him. He had sought out both Missy and Jane.

Alma thought back when he had met Pam prior. He had enjoyed the interactions he had with the flirty girl and wanted to get to know her.

"Jane and Missy don't need to learn of this for now." Alma thought to himself. "If nothing comes of this, who is the wiser." In reality Alma dreaded telling his wives of his interest in an eighteen-year old. The less they knew for now the better.

It had only taken a few weeks for Alma to get approval from the council. Alma then gave his response to Pam's father that he might be interested in courting Pam, but he would like to meet her first before deciding.

The distance kept anything from moving forward for a while. Inpatient, the two decided to start by meeting over the phone. Alma took these calls tucked away in his office. He wasn't ready to let Missy and Jane know about the affair.

Pam was enamored with the phone calls. After three calls, they had already started a little teasing game. The two joked and talked about all sorts of frivolous matters They were the exact conversations expected from young adults. The only problem was one of them wasn't young.

When Alma announced he would be coming down to Yuma to visit, Pam was beside herself. Finally able to meet Alma in person was like a dream come true.

Telling Missy and Jane he had business from the Council in Yuma, Alma left to meet Pam. He was not fully lying as he had volunteered earlier in the week when the council had asked for help on a work project in Yuma.

When Alma and Pam met, they connected right away. Upon arriving in Yuma, Alma went straight to the Smith residence and introduced himself. Before settling down at his friend's house where he was staying, Alma found himself spending the evening with the Smith family. Meeting with the Smith family dominated Alma's time during the whole trip.

After completing the daily tasks for the work project, Alma had no other distractions. Being alone and having little else to do, Alma was able to freely visit with Pam. Because of this, the relationship between the two blossomed quickly.

Over the next two weeks, Alma and Pam went out almost every night. Alma was infatuated with the girl. The two would spend hours discussing every Gospel topic imaginable. Pam knew the Gospel well for someone her age.

When Pam had told Alma she knew they had covenanted in the pre-existence to be together, Alma quickly bought into the idea. How could he not? She was perfect. She also was a pretty girl, if he didn't mind saying.

Pam loved how smart and kind Alma was. He always knew what to say. They visited almost every corner of the area in their two weeks. She loved it when he would open the door for her on all their drives.

As the two-week affair wound to an end, Pam and Alma spoke late into the night. Shedding tears with her last goodbye, Pam just couldn't imagine being without him. "Do you have to leave?" Pam said with a tear in her eye.

Trying to comfort Pam, Alma pulled her to his side and held her. This was a shock to Pam as previously he had been very strict about them not touching. This new change sent thrills up her spine. She loved it.

"No more tears my darling," Alma said caressing Pam's back. "I have already sorted it all out. In a month, your family will come up north. You can move in with Jordan." Pam leaned back grinning from ear to ear. "Really?" She said. Alma looked down at her. "I have already arranged it with your father."

Pam jumped with excitement. Being eighteen, she showed her pouty face. "A whole month. How can I stand it?" Alma laughed at the expression, and then without thinking leaned over and gave Pam a kiss.

Alma quickly pulled back surprised at himself for what had just happened. "I'm sorry." Alma looked down. "That slipped." Pam put her finger under Alma's chin and lifted his face towards hers. The two then fell in each other's arms like two teenagers.

After losing track of time, Alma looked into Pam's eyes. "I can't wait to see you again," he said. Pam smiled back at Alma. "Me either," she replied. "I can't wait to meet your family." Alma froze with Pam's remark. Reality rushed back into his mind and he pulled away.

"That is correct." Alma stuttered as he replied. Looking away he continued. "They will be so happy to meet you." "I am so excited," Pam replied and clapped her hands. Alma looked down at his watch. "I have a long

drive in the morning. I'll see you in a month my love."
Alma couldn't resist and leaned in for one more kiss.

....

Alma was surprised by how infatuated he was with this
girl. Things moved so quickly that he lost himself in the
thrill of spending time with a new woman. When Pamila
brought him back to reality that he would have to tell
his family, Alma panicked. "I will call them before I head
home," he thought. "This will prepare them for when I
get home."

Alma tried to pass off the happy news, but the reaction
from Jane and Missy, who were on speaker together,
was anything but happy. They were both upset at Alma
for not including them in what was going on. Alma tried
to explain his rationale, but neither wife was satisfied.
After ending the conversation, Alma was filled with
dread the whole drive home.

The call from Alma had put Missy on edge. Finding out
he was dating another woman without her knowing
brought up all the feelings not felt since Jane came into
the family. In that case, however, she was part of the
discussion, so she was able to get through her feelings
attributing them to temptations from the Devil.

This was different. This felt like Alma was cheating.
Alma and Missy had not been the closest of spouses.
She had learned what her relationship was, but up until
this point he had always respected her and looked to
include her in all family discussions.

People handle grief in different ways. For Jane, she buried her feelings in the religion reminding herself that Alma was the head. She was his help meet. This was an opportunity to guide her husband as he brought a new woman into the family. Her mind would not let her take any other direction. She was duty-bound to her husband.

Jane spent the time waiting for Alma's return reading her scriptures and praying, doing anything she could to direct her thoughts. Jane kept her focus on responsibility and servitude. The Group had done very well with Jane. Thirty years of grooming had prepared her for this moment. The preparation was paying dividends.

Alma pulled up to the house late in the evening after driving all day. Anticipating the fight ahead, Alma timed his return so the kids would all be in bed. In a cowardly move, when Alma arrived, he went straight into his room and locked the door without any interaction.

A common home design in a polygamous house is an added room for the man. This room is his man cave of sorts. Subconsciously anticipating disputes, this room is built where the man can retreat when things get less than friendly, which was a common occurrence in polygamous relationships. It was a place where he could have some alone time.

Door shut and locked, there was nothing for Missy and Jane to discuss. This conversation would happen in the morning.

Missy knew this tactic well. Seeing Alma resort to it in a moment like this fueled her anger. Anger was Missy's resort. It helped cover the pain she was feeling inside.

Jane spent the night crying herself to sleep keeping her mind occupied with the tunes from every hymn she could recite.

The next day was a Sunday. Alma got up to head north for Priesthood Meeting. For some reason, he felt the need to leave extra early this morning. To Alma's disappointment, Missy and Jane were outside waiting. They caught him before any escape. Priesthood responsibilities were going to suffer due to family obligations this morning. Alma was stuck having to face his wives.

"Don't you leave this house." Missy stepped in front of Alma. "We are having a talk. You are not dodging us this time." Alma lowered his head in defeat and headed to the kitchen table. Jane was not far behind as she came out of her room. A silent tug-of-war then ensued for several minutes where no one was going to lose ground by starting the conversation. Alma sat head down feeling the eyes of both women.

Alma finally broke the silence. "I know this is right. You have to trust me," he said trying to sound convincing. Missy looked at Alma with disbelief. "What does that mean?" She responded. "You were engaging in a relationship without telling us. What is right about that?" Alma didn't have a response.

"Missy, calm down." Jane broke in. "Alma what is going on? This is not like you to leave us out. You must have had a reason." Seizing the opened door, Alma took advantage and jumped into the speech he had been preparing on his long drive home.

"I felt prompted by the Lord that this was right. I was going by His direction. Brother Smith contacted me two months ago." "Two months ago?" Missy broke in exasperated. "Yes, two months ago." Alma replied and went back into his narrative. "He let me know that Pamila was interested and Brother Levi had given his okay. I didn't say anything because I wasn't sure. I knew I had business in Yuma, so I decided to investigate there before making any decisions."

"Why didn't you say anything?" Missy broke in again. "Let him finish." Jane put her hand on Alma. "As I was saying," Alma said giving Jane a nod. "I went to investigate. When I got there and met with the Smith family the spirit was so strong. I knew this is what the Lord wanted. I apologize for not letting you know. I should have, but I was following the Lord's direction." Alma paused for a couple seconds. Looking both women in the eye, he then concluded. "You will need to take it up with Him." Alma liked what he was saying and was now convincing himself of what he had done.

Missy stared in amazement at her husband. The declaration was clear. He claimed revelation, and now it was her obligation to get a testimony from God of what her husband had said. This enraged Missy. She saw right through the tactic and was not going to stand for her husband using God as a shield.

Deeper down, one of the things bothering Missy was Pamila's age. Pam was only a few years older than Ruth. Missy knew eighteen-years was a common age for marriage in the group, but now she had two daughters approaching this age. "How could Alma not see this?" Missy thought to herself. "A man should know better than go after someone the same age as his children." This was adding to the betrayal she was feeling.

It was at this point where the relationship between Missy and Jane severed, possibly never to be fully restored. Just as Missy was about to lay into Alma, Jane put her arm around him. "Thank you dear," she said. "I knew there was an explanation. It all makes sense now."

Jane then turned and looked at Missy but spoke to Alma. "I don't think you should go to Priesthood Meeting this morning." Jane put Alma's hand in hers and led him to her bedroom, leaving Missy in shock at the table.

Chapter 6
Sister Wives

Missy and Alma had kept their distance since the morning encounter. Jane and Missy, on the other hand, could not avoid each other. Over the next few weeks, the two women would work side by side for a few minutes before an inevitable side comment would send both to their rooms in anger.

Jane's actions had caused a deep wound in her relationship with Missy. Missy was angry at her husband, but Jane's condoning Alma and rubbing it in Missy's face struck at Missy's heart. The two had learned to live with each other, which had grown to a love and respect as they raised their children. She just could not get over why Jane would be so malicious in her actions.

Jane was thinking more of her responsibilities, doing everything she could to keep herself from reality. Trying to play her part, she wanted Alma to know she respected his authority and was trying to show it. In her mind, Missy should have been doing the same.

Jane was frustrated at how stubborn Missy was being. It was no wonder to her where Claire got her stubbornness. If Missy would just come along, things would be a lot easier.

All this led up to the Sunday where the family met Pam for the first time.

....

Seeing Pam for the first time had sent the Thomas family on a whirlwind of emotion. When the family returned home after meeting her, no one was in the mood for fireside or Sunday evening conversation. The kids went straight into their rooms.

Sharing the same room, Ruth and Claire talked back and forth about the day's events. The lesson from Bishop Korban had been overshadowed by the introduction of Pam.

"You should have seen mom," Claire said after the two had been talking for a while. "She is not taking this well at all." "At least we know what all the fuss has been lately," Ruth replied. "I'm getting worn out doing everything in the house."

"Ruth," Claire said. "Is that all you can think about? Mom is really hurting. I've never seen her like this." Ruth looked over at Claire. "I know she is hurting. I don't understand it though. It is not like we all didn't know Dad was going to marry another woman at some point."

The two sat in silence for a few minutes. "I will say," Ruth started the conversation again. "She is really young. I remember her from youth conference last year. She was hanging out with Sallie and Wendy." The two sat in silence again, both processing the situation.

"Maybe that is why Mom is struggling." Claire broke the silence. "I have to admit it is weird." Ruth replied. "Ruth," Claire said. "I think we need to go see how Mom is doing. I am worried about her." "I agree," Ruth replied. The two girls headed to their mother's room.

....

"Mom, are you doing okay?" Ruth asked as she sat on the bed by her mother. "I have just had a bad day is all." Missy replied trying to disguise her emotions. "Is it about Pamila Smith and Dad?" Claire asked.

Missy looked at her two girls with a sense of remorse in her eyes. "Sweetheart, there are things that happen among your parents that need to stay there." Missy replied. "We have to work them out. It has nothing to do with you kids." Missy had no desire to put her husband down in front of her kids. More importantly, she was now seeing the strain the last few weeks had been on her kids.

Claire sat down and laid her head on Missy's shoulder. "Mom, I sat with you for an hour during Sacrament Meeting. I saw your look when Pam came out." Missy put her arm around Claire. "Claire dear, please no more questions. All you need to know is we all love you."

"Mom," Ruth stepped in. "The house has been filled with tension for over three weeks. Your keeping us in the dark is not helping. Claire and I have been comforting the kids almost every day, even Nephi has come to us."

As sorrow often does, Missy had been focusing inward. Listening to her two girls, she was seeing the struggles this issue had caused on the kids. "Come here girls." Missy said.

As Ruth joined by her mom Missy tightly hugged her two daughters quickly maturing into women. "I am sorry for the pain you have all felt. I love you two strong women." This is the first time Missy had called the two girls women. Both Ruth and Claire looked up with affection. Missy continued. "You mean everything to me. I am so sorry we have been putting all this on you." Missy kissed both her daughters on the forehead.

The three women held each other for a moment. Feeling the absence of her boy, Missy turned to Ruth. "Ruth, will you do me a favor?" Ruth looked up at her mom and nodded. "Will you bring Nephi in here?" Ruth went out and grabbed their brother.

Missy and her kids went long into the night spending time with each other, mother and her three children.

.....

Three days had passed since Pam moved in with her brother's family. Alma had arranged for her to meet with his family. Pam was excited to see Alma again but was nervous about formally meeting the Thomas family.

Pam's excitement rose as Alma knocked on the door to pick her up. Pam rushed to open the door. Seeing Pam Alma smiled. "Shall we go?" He asked with a bow, and then moved to the side allowing Pam to pass. "With pleasure." Pam curtsied. The two got into Alma's truck and headed to his home to meet the rest of the family.

As they pulled into the driveway Marvie, Josiah, and Lucy were out running around. Pam's heart sank into her stomach with nerves seeing the Thomas kids playing in the yard. "Such sweet kids." Pam said to Alma. Seeing only the younger ones had set Pam at ease a little.

As they got out of the car, Lisa ran over to Pam. "Are you gonna be our new aunt?" Lisa said with a curious look on her face. Pam blushed and looked over at Alma, who was smiling. Pam looked down at Lisa. "Well I don't know. Right now I am just glad I actually get to meet you and," Pam paused looking over to Alma. Alma mouthed the names of the other two. Pam continued, "You Lisa, Marvie, and Josiah."

As the evening progressed, Pamila got along with the Thomas children well enough. Not knowing how to interact with the older Thomas children, Pam focused her attention on the three little ones. Being just three years older than Ruth, the interactions with the older kids was somewhat more distant.

After mingling for a little, the family sat down for dinner. Jane was anxious for her and Missy to speak with Pam alone. As soon as everyone was done eating, Jane spoke up. "Off to the Pad now kids with your father." Jane announced to the living room. Alma looked up a little startled. "That is correct Mr." Jane joked at Alma. "You go play ball with the boys. Us women have some talking to do." Alma and the kids knew their que and headed out the door.

Pamila did not have much life experience. Young and in love, she didn't have the forethought to think of how her courting Alma would affect these other women. Seeing them in person had brought her into reality.

"Alma is so thoughtful. Don't you think?" Pam started the conversation after the three were alone. "He is such a gentleman." "Wait until you get to know him." Missy said sarcastically. Jane gave Missy a look. "Enough about him," Jane said looking back at Pam. "We want to know about you."

The three women then went back and forth discussing everything women discuss when men aren't around. Missy could see the youth and naivety from Pam. In some ways it gave her some charm. She was not trying to be malicious or cause ill will. She was just doing what every other girl in the Group does.

The conversation was going better than expected. Missy was giving a little more slack to this innocent child. She could see the issue was more with Alma.

"The last night in Yuma with Alma was so hard." Pamila said. She had been rambling on and on about the adventures the two had that week. "He was so sweet. When he kissed me, it was just so amazing." Both Missy and Jane looked up in surprise.

"What!?" Missy halted the conversation, startling Pam. "He kissed you?" Missy said as she leaned forward in her chair.

Having an older woman come on at her like this put Pam into a defensive mode and she folded into herself on her chair. "Missy, you're scaring the poor girl." Jane spoke angrily at Missy. "I don't care." Missy replied. "He had no right to kiss her. The one thing we have that makes this bearable is the respect to keep distance during courting."

Pamila was in tears now. She did not intend to spark this reaction. "It was only this once. I swear. The rest of the time he kept his distance." "Quiet you." Missy waved her hand dismissively at Pamila. "The adults are talking now." Jane snapped at Missy. "You have gone too far Missy. Besides I am pretty sure he kissed me as well when we were dating." "Are you kidding me?" Missy said in anger. All this news had flooded her with emotions.

"Why did you wait until now to tell me this?" Missy continued. "Alma and I didn't even touch each other until we kissed across the altar. That was the one saving grace for him. I assumed I had that trust from him. Now the two of you have just shattered any confidence I could have in that man."

"Enough!" Jane yelled. Missy's chest was pumping. Missy was about to respond, but she looked over at Pam balled up in the corner. Missy turned back to Jane. "You are right. Enough," she said. Missy got up out of her chair and walked out of the room.

....

Men have been chauvinistically trained in the Group. They see their wives as subservient to them and expect them to take their direction. When the men have conflict with their wives a common tactic is to distance themselves until the wife finally caves into his authority.

Alma had instituted this tactic with Missy, which conveniently helped because deep down he knew she was in the right. He really did not want to face her.

The two went on for weeks with hardly any effort to engage with each other. Missy and Jane, on the other hand, shared the same living space. They had no choice, but eventually the two found a new balance.

Time does not heal wounds, but it does calm things down. A stalemate truce had been drawn between Missy and Jane. Wanting some normalcy for the kids, the two went about their daily routines not saying much to each other but respecting each other's space.

Two months had gone by like this. Pamila had not come back over to the house since that night. Missy knew Pam was staying with her brother, which was a sure sign Alma and she were still courting. Missy appreciated they did this without it being in her face.

"Maybe I need to give her a chance." Missy thought to herself. "Alma slipped in kissing her, which hurts, but he is not the first man I have heard that has done this. In fact, others had done far worse."

Missy had several thoughts running through her head. At the root of all of it, she just wanted some normalcy for the family. She did not like the tension in the house. Right or wrong, she knew the blame for the tension was directed at her.

Ruth especially was starting to point the blame. She had even recently quipped about the stubbornness of her mother, which hurt Missy a lot.

Finally, Missy decided it was time to work things out with Alma. Making up her mind, Missy headed for Alma's office.

"Can I come in Alma?" Missy asked as she opened the door. "Of course you can Missy." Alma replied. "It is good to finally hear from you." Missy sat down on the couch in Alma's office. "I am tired of all of this Alma," Missy began. "The kids are in constant stress. I don't want this anymore."

Alma looked at her and put down the book he was reading. "I don't want this either Missy. I miss when we all got along. It is really hard to see you and the family in such torment. I know this is hard for you." Alma stopped thinking to himself for a minute.

Missy had picked up on his demeanor. For some reason he seemed a little skittish. With everything that had happened, Missy figured it made sense, especially since the two had not had a real conversation in a long time.

Alma then continued, "but I have to do what the Lord demands." Missy looked at Alma trying to let him know she wasn't angry anymore. "I understand Alma. It just really hurt that you would go behind mine and Jane's back and date a girl without including us. If you had been up front and did it with us, I could have been more supportive."

All the color suddenly left Alma's face. Missy was taken aback when she saw his pale expression. "What is it Alma?" Missy said. "You look like you've seen a ghost." "Oh, nothing I am just not feeling well." Alma was now wanting to end this conversation and did not want to bear what was about to come. "That's not it Alma. I can see it on your face. You are hiding something." Missy replied changing her demeanor. "We can talk about it later Missy. I just need to rest." Alma said motioning her to leave. "Now!" Missy scowled.

Not sure how to move forward, Alma stuttered into his words. "Well, uh, you have to understand the Lord demands this. I had Brother Levi's blessing." "What are you saying?" Missy replied, starting to get angry. Missy knew what was coming but could not believe it. Alma lowered his head. "Pam and I were married two weeks ago."

All the air left Missy's lungs. She just stared at him for a few seconds. Without thinking Missy stood up. Her blood boiling, she walked over and slapped Alma in the face as hard as she could. She then turned and ran out of the room.

Missy's running did not stop at the house. She burst out the house and kept running into the woods. She ran and ran until her lungs could no longer provide strength to her cells. Unable to continue, Missy collapsed on the ground unconscious.

Two hours later Claire and Nephi found their mother lying unconscious in the woods.

Part II

Growing Up

Chapter 7
Gentiles

Taylor Boseman had been raised by the state since she was five. She had been passed from one foster family to another since that time. Having moved around her whole life, the thirteen-year old had never made any friends and had no close acquaintances. Being a foster child and being a little overweight did not help the situation.

Taylor was surprised when she learned she was being taken out of the city to a small rural town. A recently widowed lady named Alison Cox had entered the foster care system, with Taylor being her first child.

Entering Greenfield was like moving into an entire new world for Taylor. The small town of Greenfield was very different from the city she was accustomed. The large population was replaced by endless fields. Large buildings changed to towering mountains. The scenery was different, but one thing remained the same, how Taylor was treated.

Here in Greenfield Taylor stood out more than in the city. She had been with Alison for a few weeks, and the whole town already knew who she was and her background.

The first few weeks did not go well for Taylor. Alison was not equipped to handle the thirteen-year-old that had already seen the worst that life can offer. This led to many arguments between the two. Furthermore, being an outsider, Taylor had a target on her back. It did not take long for Taylor to have her first run in with the neighborhood kids.

Taylor was going to the gas station to pick up a few items for Alison. As she walked into the gas station two girls were in the corner getting fountain drinks. Knowing the look of trouble all too well, Taylor tried an alternate route, but in a small town there were no back alleys for retreat.

The two local girls, Cindy and Lindsey, giggled to each other when they saw Taylor. As Taylor was approaching the front entry of the door, the two girls cut her off.

Knowing safety was in the store, Taylor pushed through the girls, which only heightened the two girl's sense of pleasure. The two girls drank their sodas waiting patiently for Taylor to leave the store where she would have nowhere to run.

Taylor purchased the items for Alice and quickly went for the door. The girls waited for Taylor to be a safe distance from the door and then pounced. Cindy walked up and pretended to accidentally bump into Taylor while Lindsey cut her off. "Move out of the way chunky." Cindy sneered at Taylor.

"Look at how she's dressed." Lindsey continued the banter. "If she was skinny you would think she were one of those polygy kids." This is a term Taylor had not heard before. Not knowing what it was, she assumed it was the worst of insults. "What did you call me?" Taylor responded.

Having grown up with dealing with altercations, Taylor did not typically get too riled up. She knew how they all ended. Sometimes they ended in bruises, others just insults. Taylor was thrown off guard with this new rural insult. It got her going more than usual.

The two girls were laughing and bumping Taylor around. Having enough, Taylor grabbed Cindy and threw her to the ground. "You flat chested bitches." Taylor yelled at the two girls.

The violent counterattack put the two bullies in a panic. They were expecting a little fun. They didn't expect a response. The two girls burst into tears and ran back into the convenience store. Taylor walked away satisfied she had dealt with the situation.

Being an outsider, the backlash of self-defense in a small community comes in the form of gossip. The altercation with the two girls solidified Taylor's place in the community. Word of her outburst spread through the tight-knit community. Sideways glances and shaking heads were her greetings from the adults. The children ran away. The teenagers mostly took jabs at a distance.

Life was as she always knew it. Small town or city, it didn't matter. Taylor was the perfect misfit. The only difference now is she had a whole town against her.

....

For the Group, you must be of the literal tribe of Israel to be worthy of holding the Priesthood. Group lore holds that the Israel tribe of Ephraim had spread through Europe. From there their descendants settled America and were the country's founding fathers.

The Group claims through this pathway that they are literally of the tribe of Ephraim. Native Americans, they claim, are as well, but they tie in through the tribe of Manasseh from more ancient roots.

If one was not a descendant from one of these tribes, they are gentiles, or in other words unworthy. Being a descendant of Ephraim is not the only requirement to hold the Priesthood of course. The Americas are filled with people from western Europe, so location of descent is not enough.

In order to be a true worthy member of the Group one must be baptized into the Group. They then must have their lineage confirmed through a Patriarchal blessing.

A Patriarchal blessing is given by a Melchizedek priesthood holder ordained by the council to give these types of blessing. This person is believed to have the power through the priesthood to detect one's ancestral line. Through this power they can confirm a true member of the tribe of Israel.

A gentile for the Group has taken additional meaning over time. The word has become a derogatory word that basically means unworthy, filthy, or lesser.

The Group establishes communities or United Orders to be separate or away from the gentiles. Group members are not required to live in a United Order. In fact, many do not. When they do not live in an Order the Group would say the member was living amongst the gentiles. Not ideal, but circumstances in life often causes one to do things they would not prefer.

....

The news of Pamila and Alma being married had put Missy over the edge. As soon as Missy had recovered her strength, she packed the kids up and took them to the only place she felt would take her outside the Order. Her brother Stephen was living amongst the gentiles in Greenfield. knowing nowhere else to go, Missy and kids showed up on Stephen's door. Feeling for his older sister, Stephen took in Missy and her family.

Having a large house with a baby and only one wife made the venture between brother and sister possible. Stephen was a member of the Group and moved into Greenfield to be close to Group members, but he was not interested in joining an Order.

Stephen had too many business ties to risk being tangled in the complexity of an Order. Because of his business, he also had many friends outside the Group. Stephen was one of the few that rejected the notion of people in the world being gentiles. He stayed close by, but he liked his freedom outside Group control.

Two months had passed since Claire and Nephi found their mother in the forest. Living outside the Order boundaries was proving difficult for the kids, even if it was only a few miles away in Greenfield. The kids had been to Greenfield many times growing up but living there was like being in a totally different world. They knew no one, and were always nervous about going out, not sure who they would run into.

The children's whole life had been living in the Order. They were now suddenly pulled away from their other brother and sisters with no warning. Their uncle Stephen would take them to stay at their house over the weekend in Pleasant Hills which did help, but this different world was taking its toll.

Being a born and raised Grouper herself, Missy had married young and had little education. She still had to rely on Alma's support, which thankfully he continued to provide.

Missy tried to start up home school after a month, but with no additional hands from Jane and all the emotion she was going through, she gave up. The kids were left to themselves. Until Ruth received her license, the three kids were pretty much left to roaming the hills on the outskirts of town.

Tired of constantly walking through the fields, the Thomas kids decided one day to take the risk and walk around town. After making the decision, Ruth, Claire, and Nephi headed out.

"I hate it here." Nephi began. "I miss Alma. We aren't even close enough to the mountains to go for a hike. We are stuck smack dab in the middle of the valley." The three continued walking with their heads down, none in a playful mood.

Ruth then spoke up, "I don't know why mom had to pull us away without even asking how we feel." Claire looked up at her sister. "You know it was about Pam, Ruth." Claire responded. Ruth continued. "It is not that big of a deal. Mom was already used to having another wife come in. She did it with Aunt Jane. Why is she taking it so hard?" "I don't know," said Nephi. "But you didn't see her Ruth. I have never seen Mom like that." The three continued walking.

"Nephi is right." Claire said after a few steps. Feeling the heat from her siblings, Ruth responded. "I am not saying I am not worried about Mom. It is just that she didn't even consider our feelings. She won't even tell us what was wrong. She just keeps saying it is a matter between the parents."

"What about Dad?" Claire retorted. "Mom would not act like this without cause. You were there when Dad told us he married Pam. Didn't it surprise you? Dad is the one I am mad at. He married Pam without telling any of his kids." Claire paused thinking about what she was saying. She stopped walking. "Do you think he didn't tell Mom either?"

All three stopped. "I don't know." Ruth responded. "I don't think Dad would do that." The three started walking again. Ruth then spoke up again. "I just want our old life back." Just then a small group of gentile kids rounded the corner.

The relationship between Pleasant Hills and the surrounding towns was always fraught with tension. Early on, the townspeople made life difficult. The idea of having a polygamous community move right next to them was excruciating. There were no publications or news articles about the polygamous group being there, but the valley quickly became known as a polygamous area, which brought a lot of unwanted attention.

In other Orders, the relationship between surrounding communities was cordial. For Pleasant Hills, it was an uphill battle. The townspeople did everything they could to get the Group members to move but had no legal ground. All these efforts amplified the Group's feelings towards people in the world.

Over time, the two clashing cultures learned to live by each other. They never became friends or had intentional interactions. They just kept their distance, neither happy that the other was around.

When the kids in Greenfield saw polyg kids just walking around their town, this was unacceptable. The town kids quickly changed their course and headed straight for Ruth, Nephi, and Claire. The eleven-year old Nephi quickly stepped in front of his sisters as the kids approached.

"What are you polygys doing here? Why aren't you up on the hill like the other goats." The town kids said, surrounding the three Thomas kids not allowing any escape. "We aint wanting any trouble." Nephi shouted at the impromptu gang of kids. "Get out of our way."

The leader of the pack started to laugh. "You can leave, but not until we've had a little fun." The kids then started throwing profanities around.

There were six boys in all, ranging from twelve to sixteen. They knew not to touch the girls, although their words were as filthy to the girls as could be imagined. Nephi tried to fend them off but was no match to the older kids. Nephi was knocked to the ground several times.

The skirmish being just a block away from the house, Uncle Stephen heard the fighting and ran out scaring the kids away.

Stephen found the two girls on their knees holding each other crying. Nephi was on the ground nose bloodied and bruises all over his body. Stephen helped him up and took the three kids home. "I hate it here." Ruth said as she was sobbing. "I just want to go home."

....

Alison was new to fostering. Taylor was her first attempt. The loss of her husband had made her very lonely. Not able to have kids of her own and not being able to afford adoption, this was an opportunity to have kids in her life. "A teenager would be preferable." Alison thought to herself. She didn't know anything about raising babies. Alison had dreams about how wonderful things would be. Bringing Taylor in quickly changed her perspective.

She treated Taylor well. In reality for Taylor, Alison was the best foster parent she had been with. Being inexperienced with kids; however, did cause her to make her fair share of mistakes. Coupled with Taylor's lack of trust in people, the two had constant outbursts at each other.

Taylor had learned a lot of self-defense mechanisms over the years. One of them was knowing her surroundings. She quickly learned the layout of the town, all the kids to avoid, where to go, and when to be there.

For the next month, this tactic had worked well. The worst she got around town was pointing fingers and nods of disappointment. At school she would get taunting, but Taylor found where to hide there as well.

Today, Alison was in desperate need of supplies. "Taylor, I need you to get me bread and eggs from the store." Alison said to Taylor. Taylor looked at the clock on the wall. "The kids would be around the store at this time," she thought to herself. "I can't go now Mrs. Cox. Can I go in a few hours?" Taylor replied.

"Not again." Alison said in exasperation. "I can't go now Mrs. Cox." Taylor replied. Alison threw her hands up. "You are not being punished." Alison said. "I just need the stuff, or we can't eat. I can't get it now. I am stuck here in the kitchen. Please go."

Taylor could see the need for help and was not wanting conflict either. She just knew the confrontation that awaited. Seeing the need from Mrs. Cox, Taylor gave in. "Give me the list," she said. "I'll be back as soon as I can."

Just as expected, Taylor ran into a group of girls as she approached the store. Cindy and Lindsey were among the group. Taylor tried to zigzag her way around the girls hoping they wouldn't see her, but it was to no avail. She was too much in the open.

"There comes miss fatty pants. Nice outfit you got there. You get any drugs from your mom?" The girls had been waiting for this opportunity for revenge and weren't going to waste it. Taylor stopped as the girls surrounded her. "Still no bumps under that dress of yours I see." Taylor said pointing at Cindy's chest. "What are you a boy dressed in girl's clothes?"

This got the girls going. Taylor knew she was going to have to fight her way out of this one. Just as they were about to start their skirmish, Cindy screamed in pain. A rock flew in and hit Cindy in the back.

Claire had been sent on a similar errand as Taylor. When she saw the girls go after this other kid, her first instinct was relief that she wouldn't be the target today. As she started walking by, Claire's temperature rose seeing the new girl get surrounded. Remembering her run ins, she couldn't take it. Without thinking, she rushed towards the girls picking up a rock along the way.

Before any of the girls could react, Claire bull rushed Lindsey sending her flying to the ground. "It's the crazy polyg kid." The girls screamed, and they took off running for their lives. "You'll pay for this." Lindsey said as she got up off the ground nursing her elbow. Taylor motioned towards her, and Lindsey took off running.

Taylor stood in amazement at what had just happened. No one had ever stood up for her. "Those nasty girls." Claire said angrily as she watched them run away. Claire turned towards Taylor. "Are you okay? Did they hurt you?" "No, I'm fine." Taylor responded, still recovering.

Taylor looked at the girls running and back at Claire. She then burst out laughing. "I have never seen a group of high-heeled missies run so fast in my life." "Yeah I think one of them peed their pants" Claire responded. The two girls burst into laughter.

"I am Claire by the way." Claire said, holding out her hand. Taylor grabbed Claire's hand. "I am Taylor." "Are you headed to the store?" Claire asked. Taylor nodded. "Let's do our shopping together then." Claire said. The two girls then went into the store.

Chapter 8
Friends

Relatable circumstances brought two girls from two different worlds together. Outcasts from society, Claire and Taylor instantly connected.

After shopping together, the two parted ways. In the first meeting, nothing of importance was spoken between the two. They just laughed at what had happened, talked about silly things in the store, and giggled at each other's silly gestures. It was the perfect introduction for each other.

Backgrounds and beliefs did not matter. They were just two girls having fun. Both girls just needed an outlet, something different, someone to just laugh with.

Taylor could not stop thinking about Claire, this mysterious girl that stood up for her. Taylor was surprised she had not seen Claire in school. Taylor was in Junior high, which had students from several of the surrounding towns. Maybe that is why she hadn't seen her, but Claire was by herself when they met, so she had to live in Greenfield.

The town girls were now more scared of Taylor then ever and avoided her at every encounter. This was no problem for Taylor as it led to more freedom and mobility around the town.

Taylor started a mission to find Claire. As she went along her new quest, there was a side benefit. She had really improved relations with Alison, which was not hard when volunteering for every store run.

Two weeks passed with no luck. Taylor decided to employ a different tactic and went to the edge of town after school. "Maybe Claire lived on one of the surrounding farms." Taylor thought. She started her new approach walking the back roads through the fields.

This move finally paid off when Taylor caught Claire with a small group of similar looking kids coming from the fields on the outskirts of town. Seeing them from a distance Taylor shouted out. "Claire, is that you?"

Claire looked up in surprise and then started jumping in excitement. "Who is that?" Nephi asked. Claire grabbed her brother's arm. "This is the girl I was telling you about, Taylor." She said. Ruth gave Claire a glance. "I thought you were making it up. You actually made friends with someone in town." Claire nodded her head with a smile on her face.

Ruth now had a stern look. "Claire you know better." Nephi waved his arm at Ruth in defense of his sister. "Leave her alone Ruth. We are all stuck here with none of our friends. I am happy at least one of us has someone to play with."

Ruth turned away. "Well I'm not going to be a part of this." She then headed back to Uncle Stephen's. "Come on Nephi." Claire pulled on Nephi's arm as Ruth was walking away. The two ran towards Taylor.

Claire ran over and gave Taylor a hug. Surprised at the greeting but glad to see her elusive friend, Taylor hugged her back. "I thought I would never see you again." Claire said looking at Taylor. "Me too," Taylor responded. "I have been looking everywhere for you. Why have you not been in school?"

Claire gave a little laugh. "Oh, I am homeschooled." Before continuing, Claire saw Taylor glance at her brother. "Silly me, this is my Brother Nephi," Claire said. "Hi," Nephi waved at Taylor. "Isn't that a name from the Mormon book?" Taylor asked, hearing the unconventional name. "It is." Nephi responded with a nervous hesitation.

When younger Nephi loved his name. He would think of himself as one of the soldiers with Captain Moroni, who was character in the book. As Nephi got older, he noticed the reaction people took to his name outside the Group. To Nephi, this was a dead giveaway that he was a polyg kid.

The Group taught the kids to not let people know who they were and to lie when asked about their background. Nephi's name made this very difficult for him.

"I like your name." Taylor continued, which eased Nephi's tension. He looked up and smiled at Taylor and then looked at Claire. Reading her expression, he could tell Claire wanted him to leave now. He leaned into Claire and whispered, "I like her." Nephi then looked at Taylor. "I am glad I finally met you. Claire would not stop talking about you." "Nephi!" Claire said, pinching

Nephi's arm. Nephi pulled away from Claire and gave her a look. "Got to get back home. I'll leave you two alone." Nephi gave a quick laugh at Claire and took off running for home.

....

Claire had friends in the Group, but she never really connected with any of them. Outside her family, Claire generally preferred to be alone where she could let her imagination take over.

Now that she was away from the Group, Claire really started to feel not having other kids around, which is something she had taken for granted. Taylor coming into her life was a welcome change.

The girls decided from their second meeting to meet up at this same place every day after Taylor got out of school. Except for the weekends when Claire went to stay in Pleasant Hills, the two girls were with each other practically every day for the next two months.

Having different backgrounds did not stop the girls in the slightest. There would be times when one would say something or do something that seemed odd to the other. The girls didn't care. The oddness provided fuel to their friendship.

Claire let Taylor into her imaginative private world. The girls went on all sorts of adventures with each other. Taylor loved every minute of it. Her hard background did not let her be free as a child too often. She willfully joined into every concoction Claire would come up with.

In turn, Taylor would talk about all the different things in the world. Taylor would bring her music player. The two would listen for hours to all the different tunes. Claire would smile and laugh as Taylor would sing along. Taylor knew the words to every song.

Claire and Taylor were spending so much time together that the world around them was bound to take notice. Taylor started bringing Claire to her house. Claire was not too keen on reciprocating. This was odd to Taylor, but with her background she understood keeping secrets.

After Claire had come over a few times, Alison thought it was time to speak with Taylor about her new friend. After dinner one evening, Alison decided to have the conversation.

"Taylor, can we talk about your new friend?" Alison asked. Taylor stopped what she was doing. "Sure, isn't she great?" Alison looked for the right words to say. "Well, why did you pick her as a friend?" Alison started trying a neutral tactic. Taylor was a little perplexed. "What do you mean?" She asked. Alison looked at the ceiling trying to find the right words. "With all the girls in the town, why a kid from Pleasant Hills?"

Taylor looked at Alison confused. Seeing the confusion, Alison continued. "You know, a polyg kid." Taylor's eyes lit up. "I keep hearing that term." Taylor sat down next to Alison. "What does it mean? Is there something wrong with her? If there is, I don't care." Taylor emphasized the last statement. She had been called this when she first moved into the town and was ready to defend anyone with this ailment.

"You don't know?" Alison was surprised. "I guess if you have not been playing with the other kids," Alison said, letting her words trail off as she was thinking. "And it is not my place to just put down a whole group of people." Alison continued. "I am just not used to having one around so close all the time." Alison dropped her head knowing she was botching this.

"Mrs. Cox, you're not making sense." Taylor replied. "What did Claire do wrong?" Alison looked at Taylor. "She didn't do anything wrong." Alison had gotten her answer for why Taylor was playing with Claire. Now Alison did not want to continue as it might hurt Taylor, but she was stuck.

"To your earlier question," Alison said, not knowing where else to go. "Polyg is short for polygamous. The place where Claire goes on the weekends, Pleasant Hills, is a polygamous community."

The wheels in Taylor's head were spinning as she started piecing a few things together from over the last couple months. "Are they bad people?" Taylor asked. "Uh, they aren't bad," Alison said. "But what they do is bad. Does that make sense?" "No." Taylor replied. Alison then continued. "I'll just get to it. Polygamy is a sin. We don't associate with them too much. From my interactions, they don't like us at all either. I guess I am concerned Claire could be a bad influence."

From all of Taylor's thirteen years, she had been through a lot. One of the things she learned is people's background, religion, or status did not make them a good or a bad person. She had met some really mean pastors while being passed around from foster homes. She didn't care at all what Claire was. Claire was super nice and had been a good friend. That is all that mattered to Taylor.

"Mrs. Cox, I don't care anything about that. Claire is the first best friend I have ever had. I don't care anything other than that. If you don't like it then," Taylor paused knowing Alison hated swearing. "To hell with you." Taylor started crying and headed for her room.

"Taylor," Alison tried to stop her. "I didn't mean it like that. Of course, you can be friends with Claire. I'm just, I don't know." The last words Alison said to herself as Taylor was already in her room and the weight of what she was saying started to hit her.

....

The next day Taylor and Claire met at their usual spot. As they started walking to the fields for one of their adventures, Taylor looked over at Claire. "Claire, why did you not tell me you were polygamous?" Claire froze in her tracks. "I'm not a polygamous," she said saying the phrase she was taught when she was a child to avoid this very question. Claire looked straight forward, not wanting to see if her half-truth met its mark.

Taylor continued, "Claire, everyone in the town knows that you are." Claire did not want to lie to her friend, seeing she already knew, Claire clarified her words. "I mean I am not married. You have to be married to be polygamous." Claire stopped for a second and then spoke again. "But my parents are polygamous." Claire paused for a moment trying to hold back tears. "I guess you don't want to be friends anymore do you?"

Taylor put her arm around her friend. "No Claire, are you kidding? You are the best thing that has happened to me. I will always be your friend." Taylor stepped back and looked at Claire. "You could have told me."

Seeing Taylor wanted to be friends and was okay with Claire's background, Claire opened up. "You don't know Taylor. We don't get along with people. In the past they would throw our Grandparents in prison for polygamy, so we keep to ourselves." Taylor looked down contemplating what Claire said. "I guess they don't like either of us." Taylor said, hugging her friend again.

"Taylor, you are the first friend I have had who wasn't part of the Group." Claire said as the two started walking again. Taylor looked over at Claire. "What is the Group?" Taylor asked. "Oh, that's just what we call ourselves," Claire said. "I guess it is our way of saying who we are but keeping it a secret." Taylor chuckled a little. "Yeah Claire, I think we have a lot in common."

Thinking the two had cleared the air, Taylor wanted to get to know Claire better. "So now that we are good, can we play at your house now?" Taylor asked. Claire froze again. "What is it now Claire?" Taylor asked, seeing the same expression as before.

"You know how I said that people don't like us?" Claire said. Without waiting for Taylor to respond, she continued. "Well, we don't like them none neither. It's just that we aren't supposed to play with you." Seeing Taylor's confused look, Claire clarified, "people in the world." Claire lowered her head. "I think it is stupid Taylor now that I see you, but people might not like seeing us together."

"That is stupid," Taylor responded. "It's like no one wants us to be friends. What the hell." Taylor caught herself knowing Claire did not like swearing. "Sorry, heck is wrong with everyone?" "I know," Claire responded. The two sat down on a wooden fence marking the edge of the field. Neither spoke for a while.

"You know what Taylor," Claire said after thinking it over. "We're not in Pleasant Hills. You already met Nephi and Ruth" "Ruth?" Taylor asked, not knowing the name. Claire continued. "Oh, that's right, you too have never met. She is my older sister. Anyway, I have not kept you a secret to them. Come on. Come meet my mom. I know she will love you." Claire and Taylor grabbed each other's hands and headed towards Claire's uncle's house.

....

"Wait here." Claire asked Taylor to sit on the porch swing while she went in to talk to her mom. "Mom?" Claire knocked on her mother's door. "Come in dear," Missy responded. Claire walked in and stood in front of her mom. "Mom, I have something I want to tell you.

Please don't get mad." "What is it? I promise I won't get mad," Missy replied with a smile.

Claire looked at her mom. "You know how I have been away every afternoon?" Missy gave an acknowledging nod, but in reality, she hadn't noticed. Her life in the past few months was mostly spent cooped up in her room. "Well," Claire continued. "I met a new friend." "Really?" Missy said excitedly with this unexpected news. "Yeah, but she is not from the Group." Claire said looking down.

"Oh Claire, come here," said Missy. Missy sat Claire next to her and put her arm around her daughter. "Why would I be mad about you making a friend outside the Group? I think it's wonderful."

Claire looked up smiling at her mom. "You do?" Missy smiled back at Claire. "I know the last few months have been really hard on you, being pulled away from home and all. This is great news." Claire snuggled into her mother. "Really Mom?" Claire was relieved by her mother's response.

Missy continued, "I have been doing a lot of thinking lately. I have not been a good mom the last few months." "Yes you have mom." Claire interrupted trying to ease her mother.

Missy frowned at Claire. "I haven't and you know it." Claire was about to respond, but Missy put her finger on Claire's mouth. "Let me finish," Missy said and then continued. "We, or I need to get out of my rut and spend more time with you kids."

Mother and daughter then held each other tightly. Missy looked at Claire and continued. "It is about time we start living. It makes me happy to see you getting out and exploring the world around you."

Missy moved Claire so she could see her face. "Now when do I get to meet this new friend?" Claire stood up in excitement. "Mom, she is here now out on the porch." Missy gave Claire a playful scowl. "You mean you left her there? Go bring her into the living room."

Claire took off out the door. As she was leaving Missy said, "Give me a moment to clean myself up and I will be down shortly." Claire ran to get her friend.

Missy really liked Taylor. She was to the point and didn't mind saying what she thought, and boy she had a lot to say. Missy loved it. The three talked and laughed for over an hour.

After losing track of time, Missy noticed it getting dark outside. "Oh, it is late." Missy said looking at the clock on the kitchen wall. "You know what, do you want to stay for dinner Taylor?" Missy asked. "Really?" Taylor replied with excitement. "That would be great Mrs. Thomas."

Missy grabbed the phone and turned back to Taylor. "What's your mother's name? Let me call her to see if it is okay." "Oh, my foster mom is Alison Cox," Taylor said timidly. Missy looked at Taylor suddenly realizing a whole new side of this wonderful friend of Claire's.

"Give me her number." Missy continued as if what Taylor said was inconsequential.

Taylor loved spending the evening getting to know Claire's family. From that point on, the two girls became more inseparable. The next few months Claire and Taylor spent most of their evenings alternating between each other's houses.

The two girls were catalysts in each other's families. Just as Missy fell in love with Taylor, Alison was the same with Claire. Claire being around made fostering a lot easier and bridged the gap to where Alison and Taylor could start becoming a family.

The two friends were a healing bond that both girls and families needed.

Chapter 9
Repentance

Being poor when Alma married Missy, the Thomas house was on the smaller side compared to other houses in Pleasant Hills. The Order helped pay for the house, but it was only large enough to handle two families.

Alma's business took off after a few years of marriage. He was now doing well financially. He always Intended to expand but never got around to building a larger house.

When Pamila came along, he knew the family needed more space. Nervous about the interactions between his wives, Alma decided to buy a modular home as a place of residence for Pamila.

As he started looking around, he took a lot of pleasure looking at what was available. With Missy and the kids not knowing about Pamila yet, he decided to buy the house in private and then surprise Pam with the house when the time was right. Sparing no expense and wanting to impress his new bride, Alma bought the nicest home he could find.

With all the issues he was having with Missy, Alma had the home shipped to his brother's land until everything was settled. After Missy left, Alma prepared the land and brought in the home as a surprise to Pamila.

He even had the family sent to Jane's parents in the Star Valley Order for two weeks claiming the family needed a summer vacation. Unfortunately, Alma claimed, he was too tied up with work to come along.

When the family returned Alma was sitting on the porch of the new modular home. Their reaction was not what he expected. Jane was upset that he bought the house without telling anyone. Pam did not like the idea of being all alone in a house and begged to stay where she was at, which was Missy's part of the house.

Deflated, Alma got in his truck and drove away. "I cannot please these women." Alma said to himself. "No matter what I do, a wife is always yelling at me or not happy with how I do things. I try to do something nice and this is what I get." Alma slammed his steering wheel. "I hate having several wives." He said out loud in a moment of honesty. "Shut up Alma." He said, quickly catching himself.

In self-pity, Alma started crying. "I know I will always be getting hell. Sometimes I just wish I could know from what direction it was going to come from." Alma drove down the highway with no general destination in mind.

Two hours later Alma returned. Jane and Pamila were waiting for him in the living room when he arrived. Seeing the two women, he said, "I'll sell the house." "Please don't do that." Pam begged. "That was so nice of you to think of me. Please leave it. One day I'll be ready, maybe when Missy comes back." Alma dropped his head and went into his office. Word of Missy was the last thing he wanted to hear at this moment.

And so it was, the house remained. Missy's stuff was moved into the new house. A tale of something no one wanted, the house became a very nice and expensive storage room.

....

The atmosphere at the Thomas residence had been sad and lifeless since Missy and her kids moved out. Jane did her best to bring Pam into the family, but a gaping hole could be felt by everyone, including Pam. Jane's kids missed their brothers and sisters terribly. The kids could not wait for the weekends when Missy's kids would come over.

Pam grew up really fast in the eight months she had been married to Alma. She was thrust right into daily life helping with kids. Jane was constantly dictating to her and correcting her mistakes. To make things worse, she did not see Alma nearly as much as she would like. When she did see him, he was not the same man that she dated.

The newly wed infatuation drained quickly. Only one month in, and Alma had a stern talking with Pam about her responsibilities and following Jane's lead. Alma was always busy. When she did have time with him, he avoided having conversations. The only way to get his attention was with her body, which she freely gave until she found out she was pregnant, which abruptly halted the physical interaction.

A belief in the Group is men and women are to only be with each other for the sole purpose of having children.

Once pregnant, all physical intimacy must stop. The Group believed that physical intimacy when pregnant could lead to unruly and mentally challenged children. Some even believed it might bring children into the family that were not worthy enough in the pre-existence.

With this, Pam was pregnant and out of her element. She was alone surrounded by a sea of children. Pam felt the strain from the kids and even Jane. She knew they blamed her for Missy and the kid's departure. She cried herself to sleep most nights either regretting her naivety, which broke up the family, or missing her home back in Yuma.

One of Pam's biggest pains was that Missy never gave her a chance. She understood having a hard time with a new wife. Now being married, she herself shuttered at the idea of Alma getting another wife. Still she was hurt by Missy's outburst when they first met.

Things were going so well when they met, and Pam thought Missy was a lot of fun. Pam regretted her statement and wished over and over that she had kept her mouth shut. She now realized hearing someone kissing their husband would have been hard. Pam was also mad at Alma for putting her in this position. He had instigated the kissing.

None of this was how Pam imagined. She couldn't bear any longer that she was the cause of the family break up. If only Missy had given her a chance, Missy would see that Pam was a good sister wife. "I have to do something," Pam said to herself. "Otherwise I am not worth living." Her depression was causing all sorts of thoughts to enter her mind.

....

With Ruth and Claire gone, the household chores fell onto Pam and Jane. Lucy helped where she could but was not enough to make up for the loss of her sisters. Pam and Jane were cleaning the kitchen while the kids were out playing. Feeling the strain once again, Pam's thoughts drifted to Missy.

"Jane," Pam started the conversation. "Do you think Missy is okay?" Jane stopped cleaning and looked up at Pam. "I don't know. I have only seen her a few times since she left. I do worry about her, and I sure miss the kids." "I love it when they are over." Pam responded.

"She made her choice." Jane replied. "I can't stop feeling that I was the cause of her pain." Pam continued her prior thought. Jane put her broom to the side. "Let's sit down." Jane pulled a chair for Pam. "The Lord wanted you in this family Pamila. Missy never understood that. I hate what happened, but the Lord comes first, always." Jane rubbed Pam's leg trying to reassure her. "Thank you Jane," Pam replied with a slight smile.

Feeling she was being helpful, Jane continued. "This is why Missy was not allowed to be involved with your wedding." Pam jumped at the last comment. Confused, she looked over at Jane. "What do you mean?" She said.

An air of fright entered Jane, and she had shivers run down her spine. Her response was partly to how Pam reacted, but it was mostly that she realized Pam was not in on Alma's scheming. She was assured by Alma that Missy not being involved was what Pam wanted. Jane didn't like it but followed her husband's lead. The realization that Alma kept everyone in the dark was more than Jane could handle.

"You'll have to speak with Alma." Jane said and got up and went to her room. Pam sat at the table trying to comprehend what her sister-wife was saying.

....

The next night was Pamila's night to be with Alma. She had been mulling what Jane had said for the last couple days. Pam was lying on the bed when Alma came in. Alma quickly undressed and jumped into bed. As he was reaching for the light Pam put her hand on his arm. "Alma dear, we need to talk," she said. Alma rolled his eyes dreading these situations with his wives.

Alma turned the light off. "Can we do this another night? I've had a long day at work. Order meeting went extra-long tonight. We'll talk later. Okay?" Alma rolled over on the bed. Missy laid in bed for a few minutes drumming up the courage to continue.

Convincing herself now or never, Pam turned on her bed lamp. "Alma, we need to talk," she said again. Swallowing the nervous lump in her throat, Pam continued. "We are talking whether you want to or not."

Knowing he had lost, Alma sat up and turned on his reading light. He gave a grunt and then asked Pam, "what do you want to talk about?"

Pam sat for a minute. Alma gave her an expression with his head asking Pam if they were going to talk or not. "Alma, why did Missy not come to our wedding?" Pam said timidly. Seeing the red flags everywhere, Alma went into immediate evasive mode. Alma gave a yawn and laid back down. "Oh, I guess she wasn't feeling up to it?" He said trying to show this conversation was of no importance.

Pam looked down thinking to herself. "That is not what Jane said, she said Missy wasn't allowed." Alma quickly opened his eyes and sat back up. Subconsciously taking a different tactic, Alma got angry. "Missy did not, would not follow my, God's direction, so we did not include her. She refused to get a testimony."

Pam was perplexed. She thought maybe this was the answer. Maybe Missy just didn't want to come. Alma was trying to respect Missy's wishes. "Is that why you kept me living at my brother's house and would not let me come over? You were respecting Missy's wishes until she got a testimony?" Pam asked thinking she knew the answer.

Alma dropped his head again hoping silence would end this conversation. "I need to go to bed. We can talk about this later." Alma said, yawning again.

Pam was now getting frustrated. "Alma Thomas, we are having this discussion." She gave him a stern look. Pam did not like Alma avoiding the question and caught a glimpse of guilt in his reaction. "Now tell me, what did Missy do when you told her she could not come to our wedding?" Alma continued to sit in silence. "Alma?" Pam questioned in a demanding voice.

Pam didn't speak again, letting the silence say everything it needed to say. Finally, Alma whispered, "We didn't tell her." "What, you didn't tell her why she wasn't invited?" Pam replied. "We didn't tell her," Alma said again looking away. Pam was still confused. "Alma, I don't know what you mean. You didn't tell her what?"

Silence played a role in the conversation once again. "Alma." This time Pam spoke in a threatening tone. Alma turned away from Pam. "We didn't tell her that you and I got married." He said in a whisper.

"What!" Pamila screamed and jumped out of the bed. "Get out of my bedroom." Pam screamed at Alma. "Let me explain." Alma started, but Pam cut him off and got in Alma's face. "Get out!"

Pamila did not sleep at all that night, crying the whole night with the realization of why Missy acted the way she did. Having all night to think about it, she now knew what she needed to do.

Hearing Alma stirring in the kitchen, she got dressed and walked out of her room. Alma was up at the kitchen table. Knowing Pam was usually the first one up, he was hoping to catch Pamila before everyone else got up for family prayers. Seeing Pam come out of her room, he stood up. "Pam dear. Please let's talk," Alma pleaded.

Pam walked over to him and put her hand out. "The keys to your truck," Pam glared at Alma. "What do you mean? Pam please," Alma replied. Pam ignored his pleading. "I don't have a car. Jane needs the van for shopping today. Give me your keys." "I need to get to work Pam." Alma said, confused.

Pam walked closer to Alma. "Give me your keys." This time Pam spoke shaking her body in a yelling fashion but speaking quietly to make sure no one else would be woken. Alma reached into his pocket and handed her his keys. Pam took the keys out of his hand and walked out the door.

....

Pam knew exactly where she was going, but with it still being early in the morning, she just drove around Greenfield until the sun had come up. When she saw Stephen's car leave the house, Pam was ready to make her move. Pam had rehearsed this to herself, but now in execution, she wasn't sure if she could go through with facing Missy.

She did not know at this point how much fault Missy had in this ordeal and was nervous about how Missy would react seeing her like this at Missy's home. "You have to do this Pamila." Pam spoke to herself, gaining courage and pulling into the driveway.

Tentatively Pamila approached the door and knocked. After a moment, Ruth answered the door. Her mouth dropped when she saw Pam on the other side. "What do you want?" Ruth said in a surprised tone.

Ruth was not angry with Pam. Ruth was in reality madder at her mother for what she had done. It was odd for Ruth to have Pam come into the family being just three years older, but Pam had gone out of her way to befriend Ruth. Ruth was the only one of the Thomas kids that had developed any liking to her. The two had developed a kinship over the last few months.

"Ruth, I need to speak to your mother. It is urgent." Pam said. "I'll go get her." Ruth said perplexed. "Mom, someone is at the door for you." Ruth didn't know how to tell her mother who was at the door. Missy was holding Stephen's baby when she walked to the door. She almost dropped him when she saw Pam at the door. Not knowing what to say, Missy just stared at Pam.

"Missy, I am so sorry," Pam said nervously. "Claire," Missy yelled behind her. "Will you come take the baby?" "Yes momma, who is at," Claire caught herself when she saw Pam at the door. "Oh, hi Pam." Claire said taking the child. Missy walked outside with Pam and closed the door behind her.

"What are you doing here?" Missy asked. "Can we go for a drive?" Pam said pointing to Alma's truck. Missy looked at the truck and back at Pam. "Alma's truck? What are you up to?" Missy asked. Pam gave a little smile. "Let's just say he loaned it to me."

"Sorry Pam," Missy said, not moving when Pam motioned to the truck. "I am not sure I am comfortable with this."

Pam came back over and started to tear up. "Missy, I am so sorry you didn't know about me and Alma getting married." Pam said. Getting a little angry, Missy replied, "why are you telling me this now?"

Pam started crying more. "I didn't know Missy. I swear. Alma told me last night. He lied to me. The only place I could think to go was here." Catching breath between her words, Pam continued. "I am so sorry Missy. I was so naive." Missy looked over at the truck. "I am ready for that drive now."

Pam and Missy spent the next several hours talking in the truck while parked at the Greenfield city park. Pam told her how everything had transpired. Missy burst out laughing hearing how Pam took his keys. When Missy told Pam her side of things, Pam cried more on how naive and insensitive she was while dating Alma. Pam was even more hurt at how Alma had treated Missy.

"I am so mad at him." Pam said. "I am half tempted to take this truck back to Yuma." "That would send a message," Missy laughed. "But I know Alma. He messes up all the time, but he really is trying to do what is right in his mind." "I know," Pam replied. "That is why I love him. Sorry Missy is that okay to say that?" "Yes it is." Missy replied.

After talking a little longer, Pam asked Missy, "Missy, what will it take for you to come home?" Missy looked out the window. "Oh Pam, I don't know how I can forgive him. I am trying, but it still hurts too much to be back in that house."

Pam sat for a moment thinking to herself. "That's right, you haven't been back to the house, have you?" Pam said. Missy looked over at her confused. Pam continued. "Well It just so happens Alma has a brand-new house waiting just for you." Pam was smiling at her own cleverness.

"What do you mean?" Missy asked. "Well," Pam continued. "Alma bought me a house when we were married." "Figures," Missy scoffed.

"Well it is yours now." Pam said. Missy looked at this pregnant girl, liking her more and more, and admiring her strength. "Pam, I can't do that. Besides we are finally starting to make things work here." "I understand," Pam spoke, lowering her head.

"Regardless of what happens, I want to be your friend. Can I keep visiting you?" Pam said after a pause. "I would like that," Missy responded. Missy started chuckling again. "You really made him give you his keys?" "And I'm taking all the gum out of his truck as well." Pam snorted. The two women burst into laughter.

....

Stuck at home, Alma sat at the kitchen table all day. He tried to get consolation from Jane, but she was having none of it. She completely ignored Alma and went on her way, new baby in arms, as if he wasn't there. She had heard the screaming the night before and knew what it was about. She too was not happy about being lied to.

Every time Alma tried to talk Jane would cut him off. "This is between you and Pam." She would say and then go about her business. When Alma asked for lunch, she grabbed a loaf of bread and threw it at him.

Later that afternoon Pam pulled into the driveway. As she was walking to the door, Alma was waiting for her. Jane was standing behind him in the kitchen. "I'll be in my room," Jane said and walked out. When Pam walked to the door Alma opened it and let her in. "I am glad you are back," he said. Pam walked past him into the kitchen. Alma stared at Pam's back not knowing what to say.

"This is what is going to happen." Pam started talking to the fridge door. "You are going to go apologize to Missy." She then turned and looked at Alma. "And you're going to mean it." Then she turned back. "Missy will move into the new house. Until that happens you are sleeping on your own. If it doesn't happen," Pam put her hand on her belly. "If it doesn't happen, me and this baby are moving back to Yuma." "Pam, I don't know what to say." Alma spoke behind her.

Hearing what was said, Jane walked out of her room. "I am with Pam." She walked over and put her arm around Pam. "I'll take it one step further. You are not welcome in this house until it does happen." "Jane, come on."

Alma said. Jane put her hand up. "You can see the kids. We will cook your food. But for now, you find somewhere else to sleep." "Jane, Pam." Alma started tearing up. "I think it is time for you to leave." Jane spoke in a reserved voice.

Alma wiped a tear from his eye and then held out his hand to Pam. "Keys?" he said. Pam pulled the keys out of her purse and handed them to Alma. He looked at his two wives and then turned and walked out of the house.

....

Three weeks of sleeping in the truck with no affection from your wife can really get a man to think. Alma had attempted several times to get back in good graces with Jane and Pam, but they were ridged in their resolve.

Alma was exhausted being cut off from his family. He couldn't go to anyone else. He wasn't about to expose his shame by telling anyone else what had happened.

Three weeks and Alma started to realize the hurt he had caused Missy. Three weeks is how long it took Alma to finally admit to himself that he was out of line and was in the wrong for how he treated his wives. Three weeks.

Alma spent the last two days of his forced walk about crying and bearing his soul to God. During his time in solitude, Alma found he could not get himself to pray. Every time he tried; the prayer would just trail off into non-existence. Begging for forgiveness from God, Alma finally decided it was time to go and have a talk with Missy.

After work the next day, instead of heading home to Pleasant Hills, Alma turned towards Greenfield. Alma rehearsed in his head how to interact with Missy. They had not spoken in months. He was afraid of how she would act when she saw him.

Nephi caught Alma's truck pulling into the driveway. This being the second time seeing Alma's truck outside, Nephi knew something was up. "Dad's truck is here." He yelled into the house. Perplexed, the family walked over to the window. They all watched Alma walk towards the door. When Alma knocked on the door, Nephi looked back at his mom in hesitation. "Let him in." Missy nodded to Nephi.

Nephi opened the door and walked back as Alma entered. Trying to be welcoming, Ruth walked over and gave her dad a hug. "It is so good to see you here," she said and grabbed his hand leading him into the house.

"I need some time alone with your Mom kids. Is that okay?" Alma asked. Ruth, having just received her driver's license, looked at her dad and said, "I can take the kids to get some ice cream in your truck." Alma smiled at his daughter and handed her his keys.

Stephen and his wife Sarai were standing in the distance. "Tell you what Ruth," Stephen said. Why don't Sarai and I join you in that ice cream?" Ruth frowned. Seeing her expression, Stephen smiled. "We will follow behind in our car." They all then headed out leaving Alma and Missy alone.

"I am surprised to see you here." Missy started the conversation. Alma looked at his first wife. "Can I sit down," he asked. Missy pointed to the couch. Alma took his hat off and then sat down. "Missy, I have been doing a lot of thinking." Alma paused. "I am sorry," he said.

Missy stayed standing. "Alma, sorry doesn't mean much." Alma looked down fidgeting with his hat. After no response, Missy spoke up again. "Thank you for your apology Alma, but I've got things to do. I'll have the kids over this weekend."

Alma looked up at Missy. "I don't know what to say Missy. I really messed up." Alma was hoping for some sort of opening from Missy. Missy stayed where she was. "I don't know what you are wanting here Alma. If you want forgiveness, you came to the wrong place."

Alma looked at Missy trying to find the right words to say. "That is not it Missy. I was wrong. I, I really messed up. I got so caught up in this that I never considered you." Alma paused for a second. "Or Jane or Pam if I am being honest." Missy eased up a little and went and sat in the chair opposite Alma.

Seeing Missy ease a little, Alma started talking again. "I don't know why I let things happened the way they did. I got so caught up that I quit thinking about anyone. I not only lied to you. I lied to Pam and Jane as well."

Missy looked over at Alma. "In all this you did get a good one in Pam. I'll give you that." Missy said. She then teared up. "You really hurt me Alma, more than you could ever know." Alma started tearing up as well. "Missy, can you ever forgive me?"

Missy spoke through her tears. "You treated me like I was nothing to you." Alma started fidgeting with his hat again. "I don't know why I was so, so course." "I do." Missy broke in. "You were acting out of duty, not out of love." Alma lowered his head. "What can I do to fix this?" "I don't know if you can." Missy replied with her head down now.

Not knowing where to go next, Alma asked, "Can you at least come back so the family can be together?" Missy looked at Alma. "I don't think I can move back in the house with you."

"Do you know we have another house now?" Alma asked. "Pam let me know." Missy replied. Alma looked up a little surprised. "I guess that makes sense," he said.

Missy continued, "Pam gave me the same suggestion. I just don't know Alma. I don't know if I can ever be with you again." "Maybe one day," Alma replied letting his words trail off. "No Alma," Missy said. "We can never be together again." Alma looked at Missy confused.

Missy started again. "When I left you, I was so distraught. My garments felt like a ton of lead on my shoulders." Alma spoke up, nervousness in his voice. "Missy no." Alma started to cry again.

Missy continued. "At the time, all I could see in them was you." Alma started sobbing. "I pushed you that far? Now I know how badly I hurt you."

Missy had regretted taking her garments off initially, but she just couldn't handle it. Having them off for a while, Missy realized how much of a chain they felt to her. She had resolved in her time away that she would never put them back on.

Missy was surprised at herself seeing Alma's reaction. She was kind of relieved. Maybe it was inward comfort that this was a punishment of sorts to him. In truth, Missy could not see how she could ever sleep with this man again. Taking her garments off took away his prompting her to rekindle their relationship. This could actually allow her to be around but keep him at a safe distance.

After controlling his emotions, Alma looked Missy in the eyes. "I did this. The home is yours if you ever want it. I want you back with the family. I truly mean that. I know Jane and Pam do as well. We may never be fully together again, but you are still part of the family."

This was the most heartfelt Missy had ever seen Alma. Missy replied, "thank you Alma. Your words mean a lot. Maybe one day."

Their conversation ended when the truck pulled back into the driveway. Nephi ran into the house with Ruth grabbing him behind. "Sorry Mom and Dad," Ruth said. "It's okay Ruth." Missy said. "Your Dad and I were just finishing our conversation." She then gave Ruth a reassuring look.

Claire walked in behind Ruth looking at her mother. Missy patted the seat next to her for Claire to come sit. "We got ice cream for you and Mom." Nephi said to Alma. "That's great son." Alma said. Alma looked over at Missy.

Missy put her hand out to Nephi. "I am glad you didn't forget us. Now bring me mine. Your Dad and I were just talking about how we would love to all eat ice cream together." Alma wiped a tear from his eye and mouthed a thank you to Missy. Ruth walked over and sat by her dad.

....

One year after moving away, Missy and her kids moved into the new modular home. Two weeks later Pam went into labor. Pam insisted Missy and Jane were at the birth. A long labor later, a new baby girl was welcomed into the family.

For the first time with any of his kids, Alma insisted he be the first to hold the new baby girl. Missy and Jane looked at each other surprised as Alma held the baby rocking back and forth in his chair. They were even more surprised when Alma refused anyone taking the baby away.

Eight days later the family all gathered for the baby blessing. After starting the blessing Alma said, "And the name you shall be given that shall be recorded upon the records of heaven is Missy Leslie Thomas." Missy lifted her head in surprise. She opened her eyes and caught Pam nervously looking at her.

After the blessing Pamila brought the baby over to Missy. "I hope that is okay?" Pam said to Missy. "I love it." Missy replied, and she took baby Missy into her arms.

Chapter 10
Different Worlds

Claire was happy to be back in Pleasant Hills, but she really missed being around Taylor. The two would speak on the phone quite often, but it wasn't the same. Claire had asked for Taylor to come over, but it was too much for Alison. She was not comfortable with Taylor going to Pleasant Hills and staying in a polygamous house.

It was not until Missy went personally over and spoke with Alison when she finally relented. Missy explained the housing situation and calmed Alison's fears, reassuring her that Taylor was in no danger. Being in a separate house made things a lot easier. Two months after moving away, Alison agreed Taylor could visit Claire.

Knowing Taylor was coming to spend the night with Claire, Friday could not come soon enough. Finally the time came for Taylor to arrive.

"Can you please quit checking the window every thirty seconds." Ruth quipped at Claire. "I am trying to rest on the couch. Every second all I see is you reaching over my head for the window."

Claire scowled at Ruth and then turned to her mom. "When is she going to get here? Mom, she is late." "She is on her way dear." Missy replied. "Why don't you wait outside for Taylor to come?" "Thank heavens." Ruth quipped again, receiving another scowl from Claire as Claire opened the door.

....

For Taylor, being around polygamists was not a big deal. She had seen all sorts of lifestyles in her years in foster care. She couldn't understand why Alison was nervous as they got ready. "Come on Allie." Taylor said ushering her foster mom to the door. Taylor and Alison had gotten closer over the past year. Mrs. Cox had become too formal, and Alison said it made her feel too old.

Taylor was not comfortable calling Alison by her name either, so the two agreed on Allie as a compromise. "There's no need to be so antsy." Allie shouted down the hallway. "Are you sure you want to go?"

"I am just going to hang out with Claire." Taylor said as Allie came walking out of her bedroom. "I know." Allie replied. "I am just still a little unsure about you being up there alone." Allie said this pointing towards Pleasant Hills.

Taylor gave Allie a hug. "There's nothing to worry about. I will just be hanging out with Claire." "I know, I know," Allie said trying to convince herself. "Let's go."

....

Soaking up any time to be with their older sister, Lisa and Lucy had come out and sat with Claire when they saw her exit the door. They also were excited to meet Claire's new friend. "I can't wait to meet her." Lucy said. "Oh, you'll love her." Claire replied. Lisa giggled and hugged her older sister.

Claire leapt to her feet when she saw the car rounding the corner. "Her she is," Claire said. "Come on Lisa and Lucy. Let's go out to meet her."

Claire ran up to the car as Taylor pulled up. Taylor jumped out of the car and gave her friend a big hug. "I am so glad you are here," Claire said as she stepped back from her friend. "It is so cool to see where you're from." Taylor replied.

Alison got out of the car. "Hi Claire," she said. "Hi Mrs. Cox," Claire replied. Claire grabbed Taylor's hand. "These are my sisters Lisa and Lucy."

"Nice to finally meet you." Lisa and Lucy said. "You too," Taylor said and then went over to Lucy. "It's awesome to finally meet the rest of Claire's family." Taylor then smiled and put out her fist to Lisa. "Knuckles?" Taylor said. Lisa laughed and gave Taylor a fist pump. "I like her." Lucy said leaning into Claire.

"I don't remember the two of you." Alison broke in. "I didn't see you back in Greenfield." All the kids looked up in silence at Alison. Suddenly realizing how Lucy and Lisa were related to Claire, she looked down. "Oh," she said. Then Allie walked over to Taylor and gave her a hug. "Have fun Taylor. I'll pick you up tomorrow."

....

Taylor's first visit at the Thomas residence went well. She really enjoyed being with Claire and hanging out with her brothers and sisters. Taylor had picked up on some odd behaviors, but who was she to judge. She had seen a lot worse. For Taylor, she just enjoyed being with her friend again.

Claire had a different view than Taylor. The years of growing up with the Group influence had painted a skewed view of the world. Having Taylor in Pleasant Hills opened a world of opportunities.

Being back in Pleasant Hills brought Claire a sense of normalcy and comfort. She enjoyed being back home, but the year away had added more distance between her and the other kids in Pleasant Hills.

Claire was not too close to any other kids in the Group. Taylor was Claire's best friend. Losing Taylor was unimaginable for Claire. In an unconscious effort to keep the best of both worlds, Claire began an endeavor to bridge the gulf and show Taylor the opportunities she could have in the Group.

Claire wanted to show Taylor everything about her lifestyle. Being a dreamy teenager, Claire would have private fantasies that her and Taylor would grow up in the Group together, her mom could possibly even adopt Taylor. Who knows, Claire fanaticized. They may even marry the same husband.

Claire started inviting Taylor to many Group activities. She even took Taylor to the REC at the Group headquarters for a basketball game with Claire's younger brothers.

Taylor gladly participated at first and enjoyed seeing this new culture. After a few outings, however, Taylor could feel the unwelcome strain of being an outsider. In every activity, she was kind of ignored; in some cases, she was treated rather rudely. All of this was bearable for the most part. What bothered Taylor was that Claire started to change.

Claire was oblivious to Taylor's discomfort. As they started to do more things within the Group Claire would start correcting Taylor and pointing out the proper way to do things. "Oh no Taylor." Claire would say. "You do it like this." On other occasions Claire would scold Taylor. "God would not approve. You need to watch how you act Taylor."

When the two were together in Greenfield they were on equal footing. Neither judged each other and were happy to talk about each other's experiences. Now Claire only wanted to do things with the Group and hardly asked Taylor what she wanted or how she was feeling.

Taylor was getting more and more uncomfortable going to Group activities and started declining Claire's offers.

As this was going on, Taylor continued to get closer and closer to Alison. They had really started to create a mother, daughter bond. As Claire pulled more and more, Taylor started leaning more on Alison as a place of comfort.

....

Claire had invited Taylor to go to a dance at the Pad. Taylor had fantastic news she wanted to share with her best friend. Taylor had been avoiding Claire's recent invites, but she wanted to share with Claire so badly that any reason to see her friend was worth the effort.

Taylor was dropped off by Alison at the Thomas residence a few minutes before the dance started. "I'll pick you up in three hours," Allie told Taylor. Claire came out to meet her friend. "Is that what you are wearing?" Claire said. "Well it will have to do."

"Claire, that was mean." Taylor said surprised at her friend's remarks. "Oh, you look good," Claire said. "I didn't mean anything about your outfit. It is just there is a dress code at the dance and people might say something."

"Okay, let's not go then Claire." Taylor said. "Besides I have some great news." Claire dismissed Taylor's response. "I want you to meet some people Taylor. You will be fine. We're late. You can tell me your news later." Claire put her arm around Taylor's and headed for the Pad. Taylor reluctantly followed.

After a few steps, Taylor stopped. "Oh, I forgot to put my purse at your house." Taylor said. Claire started to turn around. "Okay, let's go back." Taylor let go thinking she could catch up. "No Claire you go on ahead. I will be there shortly."

Taylor went back to the house and dropped her purse off with Missy. Rather than heading back out the door, Taylor spent a few minutes chatting with Missy. Realizing she had been there a while, Taylor stopped the conversation. "Oh, sorry Mrs. Thomas." Taylor said.

"Claire is probably there waiting for me." She then headed back off to the Pad.

Taylor could hear the music playing as she was getting close. The music seemed very old fashioned compared to dances she had normally been to, but she was getting used to the odd ways of the Group people.

As she walked up to the Pad, Taylor was cut off by two boys a little older than her. She had not met either of them before. The taller one had sandy blonde hair and menacing blue eyes. The other had a thick set of curly hair and was a little thick around the waist.

"Stop right there." The boys looked Taylor up and down. "We don't recognize you." "Oh, I am with Claire." Taylor tried to walk past the boys, but they cut her off again. "Do you have a recommend?" The boy with the sandy blonde hair asked. Taylor looked at them confused. "What is that?" She asked. "Figures the way you are dressed." The curly haired boy rudely replied.

Taylor was starting to get scared. "Just let me get to Claire. I promise I am with her." "You aren't going anywhere." The blonde kid grabbed Taylor's arm. "Let me go." Taylor screamed, getting more nervous.

"We are here to check all dance people to make sure they are in compliance." The curly haired kid said this with a little excitement. Taylor could tell the two boys were really liking their fortune of being able to enforce the task they were assigned.

"Let me go you ass!" Taylor ripped her arm from the boy. Both boys gasped a little at Taylor, her words reaffirming she was no good. "Now you swear." The blond boy said. "Leave now and don't come back until you have a recommend." The blonde boy was starting to get animated. "And change into something more appropriate." The curly kid finished. Taylor was now tearing up. "Please just let me get to Claire."

Seeing the commotion, one of the older women came over. "Sam, Davie, what is going on?" "This girl doesn't have a recommend Sister Bransen." The blonde boy replied. Sister Bransen looked Taylor up and down with distain. "What is that you are wearing child?" Sister Bransen said.

Taylor looked over at Mrs. Bransen. "Please I am trying to." Mrs. Bransen cut her off. "Not another word," she said. "Now you go and don't come back until you change into something more appropriate. Just look at those arms." "But," Taylor tried, but was immediately cut off again. "Now go!" Sister Bransen was not going to have any more from this hooligan. In tears, Taylor took off back to Missy's house.

After waiting for an hour, Claire headed back to the house looking for Taylor. She was not happy that her friend would back out and just leave her alone.

"Mom, have you seen Taylor." Claire yelled as she went into the house. Turning to her left she saw Taylor in Missy's arms crying. "What is going on?" Claire asked. "Why didn't you come to the dance?" Taylor sat silent holding on to Missy.

"They wouldn't let her in." Missy spoke up. Claire stood for a second trying to process what was said. "It was because of what you were wearing wasn't it?" Claire said in a sarcastic tone. "Claire!" Missy quipped giving Claire a look of disappointment.

"I just want to go home." Taylor said. Missy looked back at Taylor and gave her another hug. "Come on dear. I'll take you." Missy replied.

Missy picked Taylor up. As they were walking out the door, Missy turned to Claire. "Don't you have anything to say?" Missy said to her daughter. Claire turned and went to her room.

Claire was mad all night. She filled the whole night telling stories to herself. "I told Taylor what to wear. She just wouldn't listen. She ruined the whole night. She doesn't like who I am. I can tell. She keeps avoiding my invitations. We aren't bad. If she would just relax a little, she would see who we are. Maybe she is a gentile after all and is not worthy to be in the Group."

....

With Missy moving back, the family started calling the houses by the names of the moms that lived in them. Morning prayer was still a routine with the family. Every morning they walked over to Aunt Jane and Pam's house.

Missy peaked into Claire's room. "Claire, can we talk?" Missy said. Hearing her mom, Claire sat up. "We still have an hour before heading over to Aunt Jane and Pam's for morning prayer," Claire said. "I know. I wanted to speak with you." Missy replied. Claire lowered her head. "About Taylor isn't it? I couldn't believe she just left me. I don't think she likes us Mom."

Missy motioned for Claire to follow. "Come into the living room Claire. We need to talk." Claire reluctantly got out of bed and followed her mom. As Claire sat down Missy pulled her chair so the two were facing each other.

"Did you even think to ask why Taylor was crying?" Missy said looking in Claire's eyes. Claire looked down. "Well she wasn't dressed right Mom." Claire had put together that Taylor was stopped at the dance entrance.

Missy lifted Claire's chin not happy what her daughter was saying. "Now you listen here Claire. The Group is not perfect. In fact, the Group can be really mean to outsiders sometimes. One thing I learned when moving away is the world is not such a bad place." Missy paused and then continued. "The Group was at fault here, not Taylor."

This is the first Claire had heard someone in the Group speak badly about it. "Mom, Taylor keeps thumbing her nose at us. She won't even give the Group a chance." Claire said. "Are you sure that is what is happening?" Missy replied.

Missy stood up and started pacing looking for the words to say. Missy decided to change this conversation realizing the root of why Claire was acting the way she was. Missy went back and sat by Claire. "Claire, you are going to have to ask Taylor what happened."

Sitting for a while in contemplation, Missy convinced herself to go down her new path. "You more than any of my kids felt the struggle your dad and I had." Missy corrected herself, "have."

Claire looked up surprised at the change the conversation took. "What does this have to do with me and Taylor?" Claire asked. "Shush now and Let me speak." Missy replied. "You saw how hurt I was?" Missy asked. Claire nodded her head. Claire looked down again. "I love Dad, but Mom he really hurt you." Claire said. Missy put her hand on Claire's leg. "He did Claire, but do you know what? I don't blame him."

Claire couldn't figure out what this conversation was about. She looked up questioning with her eyes. Missy continued. "My mind has been all over the place the last couple years. I went over and over how he could do what he did and be so mean." Missy paused for a moment. "Do you know what changed, when I could finally let myself be around him?" Claire thought for a moment. "I know mom. It was aunt Pam."

"Yes, she was a big help." Missy paused contemplating. "She is what restored any goodness in all this. But that is not what let me forgive your Dad." Claire looked up at her mom who was now tearing up. Missy continued. "I realized that Alma was doing what he was trained to do." Missy paused again seeking the look in her daughter's eyes. "I don't forgive what your dad did, but that wasn't him Claire. It was the Group."

"Mom, what does the Group have to do with what happened?" Claire did not like hearing this. She had not connected the Group with her Dad's actions. Missy grabbed Claire's leg again. "Claire, the Group, this culture, has caused people to do evil things." "Mom?" Claire responded with her tone asking Missy not to continue.

Missy looked down. "I am not saying I don't believe or don't have a testimony. I have found great comfort in our beliefs, but Claire you need to know that beliefs about God is different from the Group. The Group is the culture. This culture is sick, and I hate it." Missy said this last piece emphasizing her feelings of disgust.

A range of emotions was running through Claire. "Why didn't you leave Mom?" Claire said. This was not a real question but was as a jab at her mother. Missy looked down again. "I can't. I have nothing else. My family is here. I learned that as well when we moved away. I know nothing else."

Missy stood up and walked to the door. She then turned back to her daughter. "I know you don't understand this right now Claire, but you need to understand you have a choice. You don't have to live this way. You don't have to be a part of the Group."

Statements like this are never said in the Group. These words only come from sincere self-reflection wrought with a lot of pain. They are words the Group actively tries to suppress.

The Group pushes that damnation comes from leaving. Parents often shutter at the thought of their kids growing up not believing. They do everything they can the entire life of their children to ensure their children stay in the Group. For Missy to say what she said was flying in the face of sixteen years of Claire's grooming. Claire couldn't process what her mom was saying.

"Mom, I don't want to talk about this anymore." Claire said. "I know." Missy responded. "Just think about what I am saying."

Bringing this full circle, Missy concluded. "Taylor has her own path Claire. You can't force the Group on her. If she doesn't want to be this way you have to accept that and love Taylor for who she is."

Claire began to respond, but Missy put her hand up. "They were really mean to her Claire. There is no excuse for how they treated her." Missy cleared the lump in her throat. "Taylor felt the wrath of the Group. It was then made worse when her best friend wasn't there to support her."

Missy looked down not liking the hurt in her daughter's eyes but knowing it had to be spoken. Claire ran back into her room crying as she went.

Chapter 11
Complexity

Three months had gone by since the dance at the Pad. Claire and Taylor had not spoken since that night. Claire had been processing a lot of emotions and just didn't want to face Taylor. She didn't want to hear more about how bad the Group was. She had heard enough from her mother and wasn't ready for the same talk from her friend. Claire was still feeling Taylor was judging her way of life and was not being reasonable.

Her Mom's words had struck her, but Claire had concluded that what her mom was saying had more to do with her mother's hurt from what her dad did than from the Group. In some ways Claire was feeling her dad had caused her mom to turn her away from the Group, which made her angrier at him. Where the rest of the family had made their peace for the most part, Claire could not get the image of her mom in the woods out of her mind. She would never forgive her dad for this.

These were all things running through Claire's mind. In the end, she had a testimony of the Gospel. That is what she leaned on. Being around people that made her question her testimony is something that put fear in her inner conscience. Taylor, her mom, her dad, Claire did not want to be around anyone.

The saving grace for Claire is she had just received her driver's license. This allowed her to take her mom's car whenever possible to just get away.

After the three months, Missy had enough. "Claire," Missy cornered Claire as Claire returned from one of her getaways. "You have been avoiding everyone for months now. This has got to stop. I spoke with Alison the other day. You still haven't even spoken with Taylor. I know you are struggling, but you can't just keep everyone out of your life." Missy spoke as much as she could. "I'm going to my room," Claire replied and walked away.

After an hour Missy knocked on the door. "Claire, I am sorry. Can we talk? I have some other news." Claire opened the door and then sat back on her bed without saying anything. Missy came in and sat by her daughter. "I'm sorry Claire. It just hurts to see you like this."

Claire let a tear come to her eye. "I hate it mom. I am mad at Taylor. I am mad at dad. I am mad at you. I don't know. I just want to be alone." Missy put her arm around Claire. "Claire, you are figuring things out. You take all the time you need. Just don't forget there is a close friend down there." Missy pointed towards Greenfield. "She is not someone you want to let slip away."

Claire looked at her mother. "I don't want to Mom. I just can't handle what she is going to say about me or the Group." "Claire, I don't think you give Taylor enough credit.," Missy replied. "I think you need to talk with her." "I know you are right Mom." Claire gave her mom a hug. "I just don't know how."

After holding each other for a while, Claire asked, "What was the news you had?" "Well," Missy replied.

"While you have been out so much, your sister started courting someone." "What?" Claire said surprised. "Who?" Missy gave a forced smile then replied, "Ben Jacobs."

"No way," Claire said in dismay. "He was such a tease when we were younger. Why didn't she tell me?" "Well you haven't been the easiest to reach lately." Missy replied. "Ruth asked me to talk with you. Ben and his wife Wendy are coming over for dinner tonight. She didn't want you to be surprised."

....

"Wendy loves to pop em out," Ben said and he poked his wife. Missy had just asked about the new baby, seeing that Wendy was pregnant. "Stop that you tease." Wendy Slapped Ben's shoulder playfully. Ben looked over to Ruth and gave her a wink. Ruth laughed back at him. Claire rolled her eyes. "Same tease as always." Claire thought to herself.

"Mom, Ben is taking us out tomorrow up the canyon." Ruth said excitedly. Ben looked at her. "Actually, Willie, Matt, and I are going fishing tomorrow morning." Ruth looked at Ben. "Oh," Ruth said letting the air out of her lungs. "I thought you told me yesterday that."

Ben cut her off. "I did, but the guys are going out tomorrow." Wendy was caught off guard as well. "When did you decide this?" Wendy asked. "They called me a few hours ago." Ben said flippantly. Claire looked over and saw the disappointed look in Ruth's eye. "Same old Ben," she thought again to herself.

"So, Mrs. Thomas when is dinner going to be up?" Ben said in a playful tone changing the subject. "The girls just called, and I decided dinner wasn't important." Missy replied giving Ben a look.

Ruth gave a gesture at her mom to stop. Missy looked at Ruth and softened her tone. "It is almost ready. Claire will you go pull the roast out of the oven?"

Still back on the fishing trip, Nephi piped in. "Any chance I could tag along on that trip Ben?" He said it a little playfully in case Ben said no. That way he could just wave it off as him kidding around. Ben looked around. He was about to say no, but he caught Wendy's eye. He then looked at Ruth who was giving him a pleading look. "Sure kid," Ben said reluctantly. "I'll pick you up at six." Pleased, Nephi gave himself a gesture of success. "Thanks Ben. I won't get in the way. I promise."

The night went on with Ben being his same old self. He hadn't grown up at all. Claire could see all this made Ruth and Wendy uncomfortable, but they played along.

After a couple hours Wendy chimed in. "We've got to go get the kids." "Okay," Ben said and got up off the couch. "I'll walk you out," said Ruth. And the three went out the door.

Missy closed the door and looked at Nephi and Claire. "Finally," she said with an exhausted expression. Nephi and Claire laughed as Missy walked to the kitchen.

….

Part 2 Chapter 11

Claire, Ruth, and Missy were sitting at the table the next morning. Nephi had gone with Ben and his friends. "What do you think?" Ruth asked in a giggly tone to Missy and Claire. She was so infatuated with her new beau that the warning flags were flying right over her. "Well," Missy started. "He is the Ben I watched growing up." Before Ruth could reply for clarification, Claire jumped in. "Why didn't you tell me you were with someone?"

Ruth looked at her for a second. "You haven't been around much. When you have been around you just sulk everywhere." Ruth replied. Claire lowered her head. "I'm sorry. I should have been there for my sister."

"I understand," Ruth said "I know you and Taylor have been at odds lately. That has to be hard." Claire looked distantly out the window. "I don't want to talk about it," Claire replied.

....

A month had gone by since Claire learned the news of Ruth courting Ben. Claire had still not gone and spoken with Taylor. Her sister courting Ben had occupied Claire's attention.

Ruth had arranged an outing with Claire and Wendy. Ruth was pretty sure she was going to marry Ben. She wanted Claire to get to better know her possible new sister wife.

The three planned a trip to Scottsdale for the day. Overall, the outing went well. Claire didn't have any real issues with Wendy, but Claire thought she was a little high on herself. Claire was also annoyed how Wendy kept telling Ruth what to do and the things she should get.

The three ended the long day back at Ben's house. When Wendy walked into the house Ben gave her a kiss. He then walked over to Ruth and faked a kiss. "Oops, not yet," Ben said jokingly. Ruth blushed. Claire rolled her eyes again.

"Hey there little sweet Abbey," Ruth said to the toddler crawling on the floor. Ruth picked her up and sat down. Wendy then pulled the baby Adam from Ben. Adam reached out to Ruth. Seeing this, Wendy went to Ruth. "Here Ruth, you can take Adam as well." "That's right, go to Aunty Ruth." Ruth replied. "Give pregnant momma a rest." Claire looked up in amazement watching her sister act is if she were already part of the family.

They all sat down and spoke for a while. After small side talk Ruth said, "Oh that reminds me. Wendy I am not able to watch the kids on Saturday. I made plans with the girl's class I forgot about." Wendy looked over at Ben. Then Ben spoke up. "Ruth, we talked about this. Wendy and I have an outing. I expect you to be here with the kids." Ruth put her head down. "Okay Ben. I will change my plans."

Claire was part of the activity Ruth was referring to. Seeing what was going on she spoke up for her sister.

"Ben we are all planning on doing a drive for the elderly in the Order. We need her." Ben looked over at Ruth. Ruth looked over at Claire. "It's okay Claire. I need to be here."

Claire gave an angry look at Ben. "We've had a long day," Claire said and stood. "Ruth let's go." Ruth looked again at Ben. "I'm going to stay here for a while," Ruth said. "Suit yourself," Claire replied. "I'll walk home." Claire walked out the house without saying anything else.

The next day Claire went with her mom on a shopping trip. Lately Claire had been going herself enjoying driving as much as possible. Today, Claire wanted her mother to come along.

As they were heading down the valley Claire asked, "Mom, what do you think of Ruth and Ben?" Missy looked out the window. "I try not to," Missy said. "Mom, he doesn't love her." Claire replied trying to keep her focus on the road. Missy looked at her daughter. "Claire, pull over."

After the car had stopped, Missy asked Claire, "keep going. What did you see?" Claire looked at her mother. "He is just so rude to her Mom. He treats her like a maid. And then he just makes fun of her." "I know," Missy said looking down. "Mom, can't you talk to Ruth, tell her to break this up?"

"I tried Claire. Ruth still blames me for what happened between me and your dad. She said she received a testimony that she is supposed to marry Ben. I tried to reason with her, but she refused and told me to stay out of it."

Claire sat for a while letting it sink in. "Mom, you know when you told me about the Group being at fault? I think I am starting to see what you are saying." Missy looked over at her daughter in surprise. Claire continued, "I love where we live Mom. I know I have a testimony of the Group but seeing Ruth like this." Claire paused. "Mom, it's wrong. No one deserves to be treated like that. I want to slap Ben for how he treats my sister. Seeing Ruth just take the abuse," Claire did not finish her statement. She let the silence fill in the rest.

Missy started crying. "Claire, sometimes I wish my girls never knew the Group. There is so much pain for women here." Claire looked forward in contemplation as her mom spoke. "Mom, I like being here. I don't think the Group is bad. I just know now that it is not perfect. I think I may live polygamy one day, just not like that."

Missy put her hand on Claire's shoulder. "If that is what you want Claire, I am okay with that. I just want you to know you have a choice. I didn't when I was your age." Missy continued. "Claire, I want you to know there is a lot of good in the world. What the Group says about gentiles is not true. I have met a lot of good people."

Claire looked at her mom. "Speaking of which, I need to go see Taylor." Missy nodded her head in acknowledgement. Claire pulled back on the road and headed towards the store. "Can I go see her after we finish?" Claire asked. "That is fine with me." Missy replied.

.....

Claire sat for a while in her car sitting in the driveway at Taylor's house. Nervous about her encounter with her friend after not speaking for four months, Claire was trying to think of the right things to say. After a moment longer, she could not just sit there anymore and went up to the door.

Alison opened the door. "Oh, hi Claire, I haven't seen you for a while. Please come in. I'll go get Taylor." Claire sat on the couch. She could hear some arguing happening upstairs where Taylor's room was. After a few minutes Taylor came down the stairs.

"What are you doing here?" Taylor asked. "Taylor, I miss my best friend," Claire said with a tear in her eye. Alison came down behind Taylor. "I have some errands to run. I'll leave you two alone." Alison went over and gave Taylor a hug. "You need to work this out." Alison said to Taylor. "Bye Mom," Taylor replied with a sigh.

Alison gave Taylor a kiss on the forehead. "Bye dear." Alison then looked over at Claire. "Bye Claire." "Bye Mrs. Cox." Claire replied, surprised by interaction between Alison and Taylor.

After Alison left, Taylor sat down in the chair across from Claire. "So, Claire, what do you want?" "I miss you." Claire responded. "Well, I've got a lot to do, I am not much in the mood for conversation." Taylor said.

Trying to find something to say Claire asked, "What was that all about with you and Alison?"

Taylor looked at Claire with an angry gaze. "Do you really care Claire?" Taylor said. The tone caught Claire off guard and stung a little. Claire went into the defensive. "You were the one that quit hanging out and kept judging me all the time." "Really," Taylor replied angrily. Taylor caught herself from saying anything else. "Claire, I think it is time for you to leave."

Claire responded, "I'm not leaving." Claire stood up, showing her old defiant stubborn self. "You are my best friend. I want to know what is going on."

"Why don't you start." Taylor responded. "You seem to know me so well." Claire sat back down and was quiet for a while. The conversation was not going as planned. "Okay, I'll just say it." Claire began. "Why do you hate the way I am so much? Sometimes I feel you think you are too good for us."

Taylor looked in amazement at Claire. "That is a way to start," Taylor responded. "Claire, you know my background. I don't judge anyone. I have seen a lot worse; I mean weirder than the Group." "Then why have you been avoiding me?" Claire responded.

Taylor was now getting animated. "Claire, for the last while, it was always what you wanted me to do. You dragged me to every Group event. You quit asking me what I wanted to do. It was almost as if you were trying to bring me into your Group. It wore me down."

Knowing inwardly what Taylor was saying was true but not wanting to admit it, Claire responded, "I just wanted to show you what we were like. That we are not bad people." "Claire, I never thought that. Do you even know what has been going on in my life?" Taylor was now starting to cry.

Claire looked down. Taylor continued. "Claire, I think you are the one trying to convince yourself. I was your friend no matter what. You were afraid I was going to hate who you were. You never gave me a chance." This hit the mark; Claire could not hold back anymore and burst into tears.

"I am sorry Taylor." Claire said wiping her eyes. "I didn't want to admit it, but you are right. Everyone judges us. We are outcast everywhere. I didn't want to lose you." Claire paused trying to breath between her tears. "And now I did anyway."

Taylor heard the pain in her friend's voice and could no longer keep her guard up. Taylor came over and sat by her friend. "I love you no matter what Claire. You were a friend to me when no one else would be. You and Allie are the best thing that ever happened to me. I wouldn't care if you had warts all over your face and had no toes." Claire laughed through her tears at the last remark. Taylor continued, "I love you as you, and that means everything that comes with you." Claire hugged her friend. They held each other tightly.

Getting up the courage, Taylor changed her tone. "Now do you accept me for who I am?" Claire pulled her head from Taylor's shoulder and looked at her friend. "Of course I do." Claire said. "Even if I don't want to be in the Group?" Taylor replied. Claire hugged her friend again. "I'm sorry Taylor. I want you just the way you are. I promise I won't bring you to Group things anymore."

Taylor looked at her friend. "You can ask me Claire, just don't put any expectations on me, and maybe ask how I feel sometimes." Taylor paused again crying now herself. "I have missed you too Claire. I have so much I want to share with you." Claire sat up and pulled away from her friend so she could look straight at her.

"Is this about Allie?" Claire asked. Taylor looked at her friend excited to finally tell her the news. "You know that dance night?" Claire nodded putting her head down ashamed at how she treated her friend. Taylor lifted her head back up. "I wanted to tell you then."

Taylor stopped and got a huge smile on her face letting more tears come out. "She is my Mom now. She adopted me." "Oh, Taylor, that is wonderful." Claire gave her friend another hug. "I am so sorry I ruined it that night. I should have been there for my friend."

Just then Alison came back into the house. "I see the world is right again and you too have made up." She said smiling at the two holding each other on the couch. Claire jumped up and ran over to Alison throwing her arms around her. "Thank you, thank you for what you did for Taylor. You are so awesome."

Alison dropped her purse and put her arms around Claire and looked over at Taylor. "She is awesome."

Alison said. "Taylor is the best thing that has ever happened to me."

Alison put her arm out to Taylor, who came over to hug the pair. The three held each other all feeling how much they had each done for each other. Alison then stepped back from the two girls. "Now, I see a car out there and no one in it. Do you have something to tell us Claire?" Claire laughed at Alison. "I got my license."

Alison looked at the two again. "Well I guess you two need to go out and do, whatever it is teenagers do." Taylor looked at Claire in excitement. "Let me go get ready."

Part III

Celestial Marriage

Chapter 12
Young Women

The Thomas family had gone through a lot the last five years, which had brought them closer together. There were now two houses, but that mattered little when it came to being with each other. The family went back and forth between the two houses with little care.

Missy and Alma would never again have a physical relationship, but they had grown to appreciate each other again. There was tension from time to time, especially when Alma would try to convince Missy to put her garments back on. Overall, however, the Thomas family had regained a sense of normalcy.

Pamila's actions with Missy had earned her a place within the family. Her three kids were spoiled by the older siblings. Having Claire, Lucy, and Lisa around made Pamila's life as a mother very easy. There was always someone around wanting to help with her kids.

Jane's actions to stand beside Pam helped with her relationship with Missy as well. The family would never be fully healed, but they were able to take their scars and keep the family together.

....

All the Thomas women were in Jane and Pam's house cooking a meal. As they did their chores, they sang together and joked around.

Nephi and young Alma had learned years ago to avoid these gatherings. They had taught this to their younger brothers as well. Seizing the opportunity to get away, Nephi had taken his brothers out on one of their grand adventures.

With the boys gone, this was an opportunity for female bonding and was a safe place to discuss what was happening in life. As naturally happens, the conversation turned to suiters.

"I saw Carl looking at you Lucy." Lisa said teasing her sister. "I think someone is in love." Embarrassed, Lucy scolded her sister. Pam walked over and grabbed Lucy playfully. "Look at her face." Pam said to everyone. "Lucy is blushing. Lisa might have a point." Lucy pulled away from her aunt and gave a mocking angry look. The women all burst into laughter.

"I don't like Carl," Lucy said. "He reminds me of Ben." The room went silent for a second. No one wanted to take that conversation anywhere.

Changing the subject, Jane looked over to Claire. "What about you Claire? Do you have any suiters?" Claire smiled at her aunt. "No Aunt Jane. I haven't really been thinking about it." "You ought to." Jane replied. "You only have a month before you are eighteen."

Missy walked over to Claire and hugged her. "Leave her alone Jane." Missy said. "My Claire is holding out for someone special." "Just sayin," Jane said jokingly. "You may want to start thinking about it." Claire smiled at her aunt again. "I will Aunt jane." Claire said. The women carried on enjoying each other's company.

....

The Group has one expectation for girls as they approach eighteen. A single career-minded woman is simply unacceptable. A woman's role in the Group is to support her husband and to have children. The sooner a woman is in this role the better.

Women were not necessarily discouraged from working. In reality, a lot of men really like having wives that have jobs. The extra income is much appreciated. That being said, the line from the Group is women should be raising children. That is their rightful place.

The majority of teenage years for girls in the Group is spent grooming them to be housewives and teaching them the importance of plural marriage. Unsurprisingly, as the girls approach eighteen they start looking and preparing for marriage. In return the men start taking notice.

For Claire, marriage was something distant and not on her mind. She expected to marry one day, but she had a bad taste in her mouth seeing Ruth's marriage.

Ruth's marriage to Ben played out as expected. It pained Claire to see how her sister was treated. After Ruth and Ben were married, Ben did not spend much time with Ruth. Wendy was his clear favorite wife. Ben was there when he needed added pleasure, but after fulfilling himself, Ruth was left fending for herself.

With Ruth's baby, Claire spent a lot of time with her sister. Claire saw the daily hurt in Ruth's eyes even though Ruth did everything she could to hide her feelings. If marriage was going to be this way, Claire wanted no part of it.

Furthermore, Claire loved spending time with Taylor. Taylor was a needed balance to the pressure of the Group. The two had formed an unbreakable bond since coming to terms with each other. Having Taylor as an outlet allowed Claire to spend her time being a teenager and not thinking of the future obligations the Group expected of her.

All of this was about to change when Ruth had confirmed a rumor involving Claire.

....

"Claire, you won't believe it." Ruth came into the house. "Where's Claire?" Ruth said looking in all directions hoping her inquiry would be answered by one of her younger brother and sisters. "I think she is out with Taylor," Nephi said as he was watching TV. "Just like my sister," Ruth said to herself. "Out with Taylor when her future is in the balance." "I think she said she would be back shortly," Lucy said, who was watch TV with Nephi. "Oh well, do you know where my mom is?" "I think she's in her room." Lucy said. "She is," Nephi confirmed. Ruth headed down the hallway to her mother's room.

Jane was in Missy's kitchen preparing some food. "What is all the fuss about?" she asked. "Beats me." Nephi responded. "Something about Claire I suppose."

About an hour later Taylor pulled up with Claire. After giving her friend a hug, Claire came into the house. "Is that Ruth's car?" Claire asked Nephi, who was still watching TV. "Claire, is that you?" A shout came from down the hall. Without turning around to see his sister, Nephi pointed down the hallway.

Claire walked into her mother's room. "Hi Ruth," Claire said. Looking around, Claire then asked. "Where is my little nephew Luke?" "Oh, he is at Grandma Jacobs right now." Ruth responded. "Come here Claire. I have some news to share." Ruth was giddy on her mother's bed. Claire went over and gave her sister a kiss on the cheek.

"You sit right here." Ruth could barely contain herself. "I've got news straight from Brother Levi."

Brother Levi was Ben's grandfather. This gave Ben, and through extension, Ruth insider information to a lot of what was happening in the Group. When they caught wind of something happening, they knew right where to go.

Ruth took a breath. "Someone is interested in you." Ruth said not able to contain her happiness. "Oh really?" Claire responded with no emotion. Claire's heart sunk afraid Ruth was going to say her husband Ben. "Well, Ben was over at Willie and Sallie's place. Something was odd to Ben. He knew something was up, but Willie was a lockbox. How rude to his best friend, don't you think? So Ben went to his dad. Guess what?" Ruth took another breath and waited for Claire to respond.

"Okay, what?" Claire said, feeling a little better that Ben looked to be out of the picture. "Willie Allen is going to ask about you." Ruth squealed with joy. Claire looked over at her mother questioningly. "Don't look at me," Missy said. "As far as I know, it hasn't gotten to your dad yet."

"Isn't it great?" Ruth squealed again and gave her sister a hug. "Willie?" Claire asked herself out loud. "I didn't even think he was interested in anyone. He and Sallie looked so happy I would have thought it would be a while before they took the plunge." Claire was speaking and soaking it in at the same time.

The thought of Willie did not fill Claire with dread. He was not like Ben. He seemed so loving and kind to Sallie. Claire had just not ever considered him an option. Furthermore, marriage was just not something she was thinking about.

"Aren't you happy?" Ruth asked. "It was just unexpected is all." Claire responded. "I just haven't been thinking of courting anyone." Ruth nudged her sister. "Come on Claire. Willie is a good catch."

Claire hugged her sister. "I am still trying to process it. Besides, he hasn't asked yet. Until that happens, I am not concluding anything." "You're such a killjoy little sister." Ruth responded. "I know he is going to ask about you. Just wait and see."

Part 3 Chapter 12

….

Two days later Claire got the call from her father that he wanted to talk. He only reached out when things were serious, so Claire knew what was coming. Claire went into her father's office. "Hi Dad," Claire said. Alma was reading a book. Hearing Claire, he put his book down and looked up at Claire. "Hi dear," Alma said. Claire went over and gave her dad a hug. "You wanted to talk to me?" Claire asked. "Sit down dear." Alma responded.

Alma watched as Claire sat down on the couch in his office. "You are getting up in age Claire." Alma started. "And it is time you should be considering marriage. A girl your age should not be running around and about such as you do." Alma paused waiting for Claire to respond.

"I know Dad." Claire responded. "I just haven't found anyone I was interested in." Alma looked quizzically at Claire. "Haven't you had a few suiters?" Alma asked. "Ugh Dad, there were two, both your age. No thank you."

Alma sat for a second. "What if it were someone closure to your age?" he asked. "That would help." Claire responded, her body language telling her dad to get to the point.

Seeing Claire's reaction, Alma continued. "Well I've got good news then." "What is it Dad?" Claire responded. "Well, he wouldn't have been my first choice, but young Willie Allen stopped by yesterday and asked to see if he could court you." Alma paused wanting to see Claire's reaction. "What do you think?" He asked.

"What does Mom think?" Claire asked knowing the answer. Alma still had a tendency to not include Missy in things. Claire knew this and couldn't pass the opportunity to take a little poke at her father.

"I, uh, I haven't spoken to her about this." Alma responded. "I wanted to speak to you first." Claire stood up from her chair. "Thank you, Dad," she said. "Let me pray about it, and I'll get back with you."

Claire could find no objection to courting Willie, aside from the fact that he was already married. Thinking and praying about it for a week, Claire decided it was worth moving forward to see what would happen.

After the week, Claire spoke to her mother. Missy had no objections either. Claire then went and let her father know she agreed. The next day Alma gave the news to Willie.

Chapter 13
Courting

The polygamous culture creates, what we'll say is, an interesting dynamic when it comes to relationships between men and women. No one is off limits. This includes cousins.

Married men are swooned over by girls. These same married men generally like the attention and have a continuous wondering eye wondering who will be next. As there is no restriction on growing up, that wondering eye often goes well younger than eighteen.

The Group does discourage child marriages, that is if an eighteen-year-old can be considered an adult. Relationships are acceptable at a younger age provided marriage takes place after a girl is eighteen.

The practice of getting to know a girl is known in the Group as courting. Starting a courtship is a patriarchal ladder dance where a man walks down several rungs before actually ever asking a girl to start courting.

The process is as follows. The man should first go to God if he is interested in a girl. If he receives a witness from God, the interested man then starts with the leader of the Group and asks his consent. If the leader is unobtainable it is acceptable to get this permission from a council member. If the leader or council member says no, then the man should not pursue the relationship.

If the man has not been previously married, he will then ask his own father's permission. If he is already married, this is not required. If he is given the all clear, then the man may speak to the girl's father. The father may ask for his wife's input, but it is not required. The important thing is the priesthood head gives the approval. If the father approves, the father then asks his daughter if she would like to court the man. If the girl gives her consent, the father notifies the interested man that they may begin the courtship.

Some practices vary in the Group, but in general there are rules governing behaviors during courtship. The two should not touch each other until they are serious. Serious means the two are clearly going down the path towards marriage. If they are serious, they may start holding hands. The couple are also encouraged to not be alone with each other until the relationship is serious. If serious enough for potential marriage, the man and girl are expected to go to God and get a testimony that they should be married.

If they get their testimonies, then the man goes back to the Council member and asks his permission to marry the girl. If the council member approves, the man then goes and asks the girl's father. If the father approves, the man will then ask the girl to marry him with a proposal that follows a common Christian fashion.

Once engaged, the two may have additional physical contact but should not kiss. Kissing is reserved for across the alter in the endowment house when the two are married.

If the marriage is a first for both the man and woman then some of these rules are bent a little. When the courting is a plural relationship, these rules are more strictly followed as the man already has a wife.

Married women are in a constant state of stress due to this eternal matchmaking affair. Every female that is within ten feet of her husband is a potential next. In an effort to have some control, it is often the married women who are suggesting or pushing for other marriages. Otherwise, as was the state with Missy, the women can sometimes be left in the dark while her husband goes and marries another on his own.

The practice of women choosing the next wife has culturally become known in the Group as the law of Sarah, in similitude of Sarah giving Hagar to Abraham. Women often get backlash for this law of Sarah. If there are any issues, the women are quick to be reminded by their husband this was her choice.

There are a few men that love their wives so much that getting another wife is not desired. The prospect of bringing in another woman ruining their relationship scares these men almost as much as it scares the women. These men are more of the exception but do exist in the Group.

The Group, in its cruelness, has no place for these men. Pounded over the pulpit is the message of getting more wives. It is, after all, only those who live polygamy that will be able to have children in the Celestial Kingdom. Others may enter God's kingdom but only as servants.

This was a favorite sermon by council member Duane Widdle. "You men who have one wife, you need to be looking. You men that have two wives...... don't think you are made. The more wives a man has the higher he goes into the Celestial Kingdom. DO NOT BE SATISFIED WITH TWO!"

There is no choice when it comes to eternity. What a religion indeed.

....

Willie Allen dearly loved his wife Sallie. The two were only separated by months in age. Young and in love, he and Sallie had the most amazing courtship and just clicked from the very beginning. They were everything wished for in a youthful romance.

The two had been married four years and had two future priesthood holders in the making. That is, they had two little boys. It was just a year prior that Willie and Sallie finished their house on the land deeded to him from the Order. The land was adjacent to Willie's parents, which gave him all the equipment he needed.

Willie and Sallie were a blossoming couple greatly enjoying their coming of age. Polygamy seemed somewhat distant to Willie. It was something he knew he would do some day but living it was years in the future. This allowed him to enjoy his wife and his religion at the same time.

Sallie was groomed to live polygamy. Sallie didn't really know how Willie felt. All she knew was if they were going to live plural marriage Sallie was going to make sure it was with someone she liked and could get along with.

Sallie had been keeping an eye for a girl that would be a good fit for the family. She quickly latched onto Claire. Sallie thought back to when they were kids. Claire was always so nice and caring.

A lot of girls look right past the second wife and are only interested in the man. This is something Sallie did not want to deal with. The thing that really caught Sallie's eye was Claire did not seem to be seeking for a husband. She just enjoyed life.

Sallie had been secretly watching Claire for about a month. At the group outing a few weeks prior, Claire sat next to Willie and Sallie. Not once did Claire come across as flirtatious. Claire had a casual conversation with her and Willie with no signs of side glances or hidden agendas.

Sallie found no red flags in Claire. In fact, Sallie had never seen a girl as composed as Claire was at her age. If she was going to live polygamy, Sallie could do it with Claire.

Sallie knew she would have to act fast. Claire was only a month from eighteen. Most girls were already spoken for by her age and were married right as they transitioned into adulthood.

....

Part 3 Chapter 13

In public when speaking about polygamy, women are openly supportive of polygamy. It is a common practice to have a woman who can't stand her sister wife get up in testimony meeting and praise her sister wife. The woman will go on to bear her testimony about how grateful she is for the principle of polygamy.

In private conversations, you will never hear them say a bad word about the practice itself. In reality; however, the pain and sorrow are deep. All women know the pains of polygamy but never openly speak about it. The truth lies in an unspoken language had among the women.

A tone or certain phrase will be uttered. Intuitively the women will know what is being said. The women will complain amongst themselves about something completely irrelevant, all knowing what they were really saying.

This language is not intentional. It was bred from the subjective stress of a patriarchal system forcing women into the literary underground. The men are completely oblivious to this. The women never speak of or acknowledge it exists.

This was the conversation that started between Sallie and her mother Laura.

....

Willie and Sallie had a date planned in the evening. Sallie's mother had agreed to watch the kids and had arrived early to spend time with her daughter. Tonight,

Sallie was going to bring up Claire. She had been nervous all day.

"Mom, how do you think he will react?" Sallie asked her mother. "I'm nervous he has someone else in mind that I won't like." "He loves you dear," Laura replied. "Make sure to remind him of this."

"I know Willie is a good man, and I trust his judgement. I just have a witness of Claire." Sallie said looking out the window. "I am grateful for the Law of Sarah," her mother replied. "A woman must give the wife to her husband, or else she will be damned." Sallie cut her mom off. "I hate that scripture mom." "I don't like it either." Laura continued. "But if it must be that way, it is important us women take the lead."

Sallie turned back towards the window. "I know we are a helpmeet for our husbands, but we shouldn't have to give someone we don't like." Laura walked over and put her arm around her daughter. "He will see it your way dear. Being a helpmeet means you can help steer him in the right direction." Laura said this looking towards Sallie's bedroom. Sallie nodded to her mother.

Willie's truck could be heard coming up the driveway. "Thank you, Mom, for watching the kids tonight. I need this time to spend with my husband." Laura did not reply in words. The subtle shift of her eyebrow responded she knew exactly what Sallie was saying.

....

Contrary to what most people think, the men in the Group are very well read when it comes to the scriptures and church history. Where the mainstream Church members are someone oblivious to their history, the Group takes it as a badge of pride to know the most minute details.

In most cases, the church history aligns very closely with the Group's beliefs. This is why the Group sees themselves as fundamentalists. They try to live everything taught by the men of old.

The men geek out over discussing the gospel. Because of this, almost all casual conversation in the Group ultimately goes to some form of the Group's doctrine. As natural as talking about the weather, Willie was going into this casual conversation with his wife. With two kids, Willie and Sallie did not get away too often. Willie was enjoying this time alone with his wife.

"Priesthood meeting was really great last night." Willie said looking at Sallie over the table. "Brigham Young is a lot more of a prophet than people realize."

"I agree," Sallie responded, glad the conversation was on Brigham Young knowing this would work into what she wanted to discuss. Brigham Young, after all, was the prophet that brought polygamy into everyday life in the Church.

Sallie started trying to steer the conversation. "How many wives did Brigham Young have?" She asked. "I think it was around 50." Willie replied contemplatively.

"How high up the Celestial Kingdom do you think he got?" Willie continued thinking deeply.

"That is crazy. How may wives do you think you will have?" Sallie responded. This is a test question of sorts for women to gauge where their husband's interests in polygamy. Thankfully Willie Answered appropriately. "I don't know, I haven't really given it much thought."

Willie quickly changed the conversation. "Work was crazy today." Willie was not liking the conversation turning personal and wanted to now talk about anything else.

"Willie, this is important." Sallie said, bringing the conversation back on track. "I have something I wanted to discuss." "Okay?" Willie responded a little uneasy where this was going. Sallie took a breath. "I think we should start thinking about plural marriage." She said, looking for how Willie would respond.

"What do you mean?" Willie responded. "I didn't know we were looking right now." Sallie reached her hand across the table to her husband. "You know we have to live plural marriage someday. When the right person comes along. I think we should move forward. Don't you?"

"I do." Willie was trapped in his response. "Will, is there anyone you are thinking about?" Sallie asked. Willie looked down. "Not really. I haven't given it much thought to be honest."

Sallie was relieved with his response. "I think I may have found someone that will fit our family." "Really, who?" Willie asked. Willie had no choice but to be interested in this conversation. "What do you think about Claire Thomas?" Sallie replied holding one eye half shut. She nervously waited for his reaction.

Willie sat for a while thinking about it. There were worse girls Sallie could choose. Willie hated it when girls started flirting with him. He mostly tried to avoid the other side of the fence for this reason. He always thought most of the girls were fake and not authentic. Thinking about it, he never saw this in Claire. She could actually be a good fit.

"Willie?" Sallie prodded, not being able to read anything from her husband. Willie grabbed Sallie's hand "I think we should pray about it, but yeah I think she may be worth asking about." Sallie smiled. "I agree," she said. "We can pray about it tonight. With the kids gone I have more surprises for you." Sallie leaned in and kissed her husband.

....

A few weeks after Willie and Sallie discussed Claire, Willie received the news that Claire had agreed to start a courtship. Excited with the news, Willie and Sallie started planning for the first date.

The first date when polygamy is involved is a delicate affair. Should the first date be with just the man and woman or does the first wife come along? Do they go out somewhere or do they have an event at the family's house? The decision on the first date can tell a lot about whether the relationship is about getting a new wife for the man or bringing a new wife into the family.

For Willie, it was the latter. With it being a first date, Willie and Sallie did not think having the kids around was a good idea. An evening picknick in the mountains was what Willie and Sallie decided upon. The two wanted to make a good impression on Claire. They wanted to start the relationship where they could see how well they all interacted with each other.

Sallie had gone through great efforts to make an elaborate meal for the evening. The kids were spending the night with their grandma. Everything ready, the two left to pick up Claire.

The first date between the three went very well. As is typical in a Group courting 'ménage à trois' most of the conversation was between Sallie and Claire. Willie sat back and let the two women talk. He would join in here and there, but mostly he was just glad to see Sallie and Claire get along so well.

With Sallie being four years older, the two did not have a lot of interaction growing up. This led to a lot of discussions on how each perceived memorable events over the years.

Claire was glad to see that Willie was not like Ben. She could see that Willie truly loved and respected Sallie. He was also very respectful to Claire. Unlike Ben, Willie would let her speak her mind and wasn't ruffled if Claire had a different opinion.

The first date being a success, Claire and Willie agreed to go out again the next weekend. This time it would be just the two of them.

....

The courtship between Claire and Willie was an exceptional time for Claire. Outings alternated between Willie alone and being a threesome with Sallie. The three did all sorts of activities and would spend hours talking about the frivolous things of the world and having in-depth discussions about the Gospel.

Claire absolutely loved Willie's two boys. They were always so excited when Claire was around. Claire would bring the boys over to the Thomas house where they would spend hours playing with Pam's kids.

In all of this, Willie was the charmer, but was always respectful to Claire. Claire fit in well with Willie and Sallie. The three appeared to show all the potential of how a plural marriage can be an uplifting and heavenly affair.

....

Something to note before continuing with the story is the affect dating has on men in the Group. These men in general have an ability to make brown grass look green when they are dating the opposite sex.

Somehow, they know just what to say, are just funny enough, just serious enough, and have just enough swagger to sweep the maiden off her feet. This is likely an evolutionary trait developed over thousands of years. Perhaps it is due to the men already having a wife, but in polygamy, these Darwinist abilities are heightened to their maximum.

Couple this with the high demand to enter polygamy and the men turn into the best picture of themselves. Truly getting to know each other is next to impossible.

This is not to say Willie was a bad person or was lying to Claire. The dating mode was just a cover that didn't allow true feelings to be expressed. Had the screen not existed, a lot of future heart ache may have been avoided.

....

Willie and Claire had been courting for three months, which was an unusually long time within the Group. Claire did not mind as she had no desire to rush into marriage.

Ruth had come over to Missy's house. This was becoming a more common event as Ruth was getting tired of being alone with her baby all the time. This was no issue for Missy as she loved having her grandson around.

"I have some news." Missy said as she sat in the living room with her two oldest daughters. "Your dad and I had a good conversation with a certain someone." Missy gave a wink to Claire.

"Oh, you are so ridiculous," Ruth chimed in. "Isn't Willie taking you out tonight Claire?" Missy said ignoring Ruth. "He is." Claire replied. Claire's eyes widened as she started putting the pieces together. "Mom, are you implying something will happen or are you just torturing me?" Claire said playfully at her mother.

"I swear, you and Willie are so inappropriate. Your flirting is getting a little annoying." Ruth chimed in again. Seeing how good the relationship Claire was having with Willie had sparked some inner jealousy within Ruth. This had sent her constantly sending mildly inappropriate jabs at her little sister.

Ignoring Ruth, Claire continued. "Mom, is he going to ask me to marry him tonight?" Claire was getting excited and prodded at her Mom for more information. Missy smiled and kept silent.

"Mom?" Claire said, getting a little annoyed. "Well you didn't hear anything from me. You'll just have to wait and see." Missy said to Claire with another playful wink. Ruth rolled her eyes and started to speak. Missy cut her off. "Ruth," Missy said. "Stop talking and give me that grand baby of mine."

The rest of the afternoon Claire was a nervous wreck. The evening could not come fast enough. Finally the time had come. Claire did not have to look out the window. She had her siblings keeping watch.

"Claire, its Wiiiilllliiee," young Missy said. Claire's other siblings all chimed in following suit. They all giggled and ran to Claire. Claire gave them a playful angry face and chased them away.

Turning her attention to the door, Claire tried to act as normally as she could. Willie came up and knocked on the door. Too nervous to move, Claire looked at her mother. Missy smiled and went over and answered the door. "Are those flowers for me?" Missy smiled as she gave Willie a hug.

Being a gentleman Willie pulled a flower out of the bouquet and gave it to his potential future mother in law. Missy turned and smiled at Claire and moved from the door allowing her to exit out the house. Claire gave her mom a hug in passing.

"Thank you for the flowers Willie." Claire said. "You haven't told me what we have planned tonight." "It's a surprise," Willie responded and opened the truck door for Claire.

As they were heading on their journey, Willie took an unexpected turn. "We haven't gone this way before." Claire looked questioningly at Willie. "I told you, it's a surprise" Willie said. "Now just enjoy the drive."

Willie was taking Claire to the top of the canyon so they could catch the sunset from the summit of the mountain. They headed up the windy road until it came to a sudden end in front of a trailhead.

"Hurry Claire, the sun is going down." Willie said. The two rushed to the top of the mountain right as the sun was cresting over the next mountain way off in the distance. "It's so beautiful," Claire gasped. Seeing Willie was not next to her she turned around. Willie was looking up at her on one knee.

Chapter 14
The Closet

The wedding was only a few days away. In the Group's version of a bachelor party, Willie was out target shooting with his best friend Ben.

"This is so great Willie," Ben said. "We dreamed of this since we were kids. We both wanted five wives. I took the plunge and you are now starting your journey." Willie fired his rifle then got up to reload. "Is it worth it Ben?" Willie said despondently.

"What are you saying?" Ben said looking sideways at his friend. Willie didn't look up. He just continued to load more rounds into his AR. "Well, Sallie and I have it really good right now." Willie said. "I love her Ben. I am hating what this is doing to her."

Ben put down is rifle. "Willie, we both know you need this for you to have Sallie in the Celestial Kingdom. Wasn't it her that told you to ask about Claire?" Willie now put down his gun and looked up at Ben. "Well, yes I suppose." Willie leaned on the hood of his truck. "I honestly wasn't thinking about another wife. I was kind of dreading it."

"Come on Willie." Ben started to reply but Willie spoke over him. "Ben how do you love more than one wife?" Ben picked up his AR and cocked it. "What does love have to do with it?" Ben smiled at Willie. Willie wasn't amused. "Don't you love your wives?" Willie asked.

Ben pointed his gun down range and fired a couple rounds. Still looking down range, Ben responded. "Well I had been wanting Ruth since she was thirteen. She was so hot. Now she just nags me all the time. Wendy drives me nuts. There is not a moment when they don't give me grief." Ben then unloaded the rest of his rounds.

Willie waited for Ben to finish. "I thought you were trying to convince me?" Willie said in a half jabbing tone. Ben put his rifle down on the truck no longer smiling. "These are the sacrifices God demands Willie." Ben said looking straight at Willie. "You know how it is. You don't gain a testimony of plural marriage until you live it."

Willie now put his gun down. "We have heard that since we were kids. What does it mean?" Willie asked. Ben put on a smile again. "Well I could tell you, but you will figure it out." Ben said with a wink. "Are you referring to having sex a lot?" Willie asked. Ben just kept smiling at Willie. "Dude you're a prick." Willie continued and started laughing.

Ben then replied. "Well, I get nagged so much something has to be good. That is until they are all pregnant at the same time. Then it really is hell." Both fell on the truck laughing.

"Now one last thing before I blast that target," Ben said pointing at the bottle 200 yards away. "You know this is the right thing to do. Sallie's eternal wellbeing depends on it."

Willie looked down range and then back at Ben. "You didn't answer my original question" Willie said. "Do you love your wives?" Ben lowered his head getting a little agitated. "I told you bro, love has got nothing to do with it. Be the priesthood leader. Lead your family. Your wives will follow. Now shut up and let's shoot."

....

Returning from target shooting in the hills, Willie got out of his truck and went to put his guns away. He stopped when he saw Sallie rounding the corner. His instinct caught him by surprise. Willie had a sudden urge of dread and slipped behind the truck so that Sallie could not see him.

Willie had been hiding his emotions ever since he asked Claire to marry him. For some reason when the words came out, they didn't make him happy. It was almost a dread.

As Willie hid from his wife, a sudden burst of reality sent a chill down his spine. "I don't want this." Willie said to himself. Deflated in his moment of self-honesty, Willie sat on the ground next to his truck.

Willie sat by the truck for a good hour in a fog before he realized Sallie never sought him out. "She must have seen me in the truck." Willie thought to himself. "I better see what's up." Willie got up and went looking for Sallie.

Willie found Sallie out by the barn and started towards her but noticed she was crying. "Sallie?" Willie walked up slowly. "What is it?" Sallie, noticing Willie, quickly tried to change her disposition. "Oh, hi dear," Sallie said. "I was just tired and resting for a second. Is there something you needed?" "No, I am good," Willie stammered. "Actually, I need to say something." Sallie wiped her eyes. "What is it dear?"

Looking around to make sure the two could not be heard, Willie pulled Sallie into the barn. Hesitantly and with nervous anticipation, Willie jumped right in. "Honey, we don't have to do this." Willie started. "Is it really what the Lord wants?" Sallie looked at Willie confused. "What are you saying?" She asked. Willie did not respond, which gave Sallie the moment she needed to realize what Willie was saying.

"Don't you dare." Sallie said. "You promised me before we got married that you would live celestial marriage. This is our chance. Don't you back out now." Willie got a little defensive. "Why were you just crying then?" Willie responded.

"Can't I have some time to myself." Sallie said, another tear coming to her eye. "That's what us girls do. We cry. Sometimes we don't need others prying into our feelings. Are you happy now?" Sallie started crying again.

When a girl is raised her whole life trained that polygamy must be lived, jealousy is a wicked thought. To be faced with the reality of actually living plural marriage sends unimaginable consternation in one's head. This is what Sallie was crying about.

Countless times women have gone through these emotions, defending the religion at all costs and then bathing in tears as they are forced to watch her husband commit God-sanctioned adultery. To an outsider, this would be total nonsensical, but this is the burden of a woman in the Group, having feelings and being told you are wicked for having them.

"Why are we doing this?" Willie said, getting back to the topic. This time there was a little more emotion in his voice and a slight tear in his eye. Seeing her husband's change in tone, Sallie responded. "I told you this is what we are supposed to do. Don't hold us back from the celestial kingdom Willie Allen." Willie lowered his head. "Sorry dear, I know you are right, I just don't want you to be hurt."

"Will you are the Priesthood head." Sallie responded. "I shouldn't be having to tell you the right thing to do." This was a jab at her husband. Sallie was not sure why she was coming across so harshly. Deep down Sallie was really hurting. She was stuck in this situation and could not let her true feelings known. His offering a way out only drove those emotions deeper.

"No more talking." Sallie said. She had already been dealing with the situation and did not want to be pushed any further. She turned and walked out of the barn. Willie kicked the straw on the ground as he watched Sallie walk away.

....

Knowing nowhere else to go, Willie went to his childhood place of safety. Willie's house was on the property adjacent to his fathers. The barn where Sallie and Willie were talking was on Willie's father's property. Beyond the barn was an old empty shed. This was Willie's childhood place of refuge. Willie spent many hours contemplating the world in this place growing up. Willie called the shed his closet. This is where he could spill his deepest feelings to God. Willie now found himself once again in this place of comfort.

"I don't want to do this." Willie burst into tears. Willie then went into a monologue to himself pacing around the shed. "My marriage was happy; my two kids were happy. I wasn't looking for another wife. Why won't everyone just leave us alone? Sallie is hurting. Why won't she stop this? Mom, Dad, Brother Jacobs all are saying this is good. Why am I alone?"

Willie fell to his knees and put his hands over his eyes. His years of grooming from the Group now kicked in. Willie started thinking to himself. "The problem is me. I need to fight the devil and turn and do what was right."

Willie's thoughts drifted to all his spiritual experiences in the past. As he was thinking, Willie started talking to himself again. "That eight-year-old was young but knew back then. Buried below," Willie was speaking of baptism. "I rose again. Confirmed a member, I held the course. A boy indeed and mistakes I made, but something in me knew this was true."

Willie's chest was pounding as adrenaline started coursing through him. "Pass nine more years," Willie continued. "The first chapter read many times and finally that sacred book I did consume. And at the end the challenge came to know for sure indeed. Get your testimony. The call rang many Sunday past, but now the gauntlet laid, I had to know for sure. 'Test me' the book did dare 'and know if what I say is true.' And so, I did as it declared and proved the words to be as so challenged."

Willie laid on the ground. Calming down a bit, he thought of how he gained a testimony of the scriptures. "A summer Sunday with no food, prepared as I could be. I headed up the mountain side, in faith, knowing God would prove the book for sure. An hour past of praying and an hour past once more. Enos as my guide, silence would not take me down.

At last at dark, a failure I felt indeed. And home I went hurt that what I knew God had not seen fit to show. I knew I was weak. What had I done wrong? In sorrow, the television I laid my brain. And in that instant when the cathode ray did ring, I felt the spirit leave. From head to toe my body drained and suddenly all clear.

The Lord had given me the answer. I knew to not look for a sign, but weak was me. I sign I had surely been in want. The answer was within. Thankyou God that it took the World to show me you are there, and the Book of Mormon is true."

Willie was now sobbing remembering that feeling. "Until that point, I had the faith, but now I knew what the feeling was. A burning some had said, well not to me. Silence, peaceful, calm it truly was. So sensitive indeed that the very energizing of copper could seize it all away. Wicked world, this is what your technology does. Now I knew, now I knew. Joseph's stone or Oliver's rod, the power truly I could see."

Willie sat up soaking in the cherished memories. His thoughts then drifted to his next spiritual experience.

"Now four more years ahead and Sallie came to me. We had known each other since we were kids. She was dating someone else and I just knew their courtship would not last. Something inside me let me know she was mine.

When all felt right, I went to Brother Levi and then to her father. He could see determination from this shy introverted frame. Yes, she said and so it went, a courtship, and what's more a friend.

We were wise the two of us. We wanted to be sure and not let the outside influence of love, passion, feelings, and the devil hide from us the truth of whether we were eternal partners. Something said to both of us we knew each other in the pre-existence, but we couldn't let our guard drop in the slightest way.

We did not kiss, we did not hug, heck until a month before we were engaged, we had never touched. We got close enough that it was time to know. We felt our passions growing deep. We decided then and there we would not speak or see each other until God had witnessed that we were meant to be. And so it was we separated.

Two weeks of preparation, careful eating, careful seeing, careful planning. Following Brother Levi's words, I fasted for three days. No food to fill. No water to quench. Only that quiet spirit to nourish my soul. I was on such a note that even the church missionaries felt the beckoning and payed me a visit. God was there all around me.

To the mountains, letting the spirit guide, I went. Oh, how lovely was that morning. Praying my soul, feeling the light. A mother deer and baby entering my presence, not knowing what to do. Their mind said be fearful, but fear was not there. We parted, our souls speaking that Adamic language, that piercing language of the soul.

And there I knelt, my words yours. God, I will treat her well. The fire suddenly coursed through my veins. The burning flame taught me another level of God's spirit. The sun was at my back, but this light was beyond description coming from in front of me. What words do I use? A Freight train of emotion, uncontrollable. God, please stop. I get it. I have received your message. You are ok with our being together."

Willie was heaving with emotion again. He stood up and started pacing again. Willie looked to the heavens. "Then why God do you demand another? Weren't we good enough? Why do the celestial keys need more than four hands to turn? Is Ben right? Is love nothing to you? I see now the sacrifice it takes to enter into your presence. Why so hard? Why?" Willie clenched his fists screaming the last words.

After exhausting himself with emotion, Willie sat back down. After sitting for several minutes silencing his thoughts, an idea crossed his mind. "I know why I must marry Claire. If I am to have Sallie, I must sacrifice everything, even her." Willie stood up. It was starting to make sense to him now. "This is why plural marriage is so essential."

A light went on in Willie's head. He had now rationalized how he could enter into plural marriage. "I finally really understand what it means to have a testimony of plural marriage." Willie said to himself. "God requires the sacrifice of everything to get into heaven. I will do as God commands."

Not wanting to leave just yet. Willie laid on the ground relishing in his new-found wisdom.

....

"No one has seen him for hours." Sallie said to Claire. Claire had just come over on an errand and wanted to meet with her future family for a few minutes. "I think he is behind the barn." Sallie said, thinking of her last encounter with Willie. Inwardly Sallie was feeling bad, thinking she had been too harsh. She wanted badly now to find Willie and apologize.

The two women headed to the barn. "Willie, are you around?" Claire shouted to the barn. "I am back here," Willie replied. Sallie and Claire went behind the barn to find him.

When they rounded the corner, Willie had a strange smile on his face. "You have a smile but look as though you have been crying. Is everything ok?" Claire said as she walked over to Willie.

Desperately wanting to be alone with her husband, Sallie turned to Claire. "Please Claire, I need to be with my husband. Can you come back in a few hours?"

Seeing the pleading in Sallie's eyes, Claire knew this was not the right time for her to be there. "How about I come by tomorrow?" Claire said and headed back home.

Sallie grabbed Willie's hand and led him to an old shed she could see around the corner.

Chapter 15
Preparations

The Thomas family was gathered in Jane's living room reminiscing about old times. This was a last hooray of sorts the family was having with Claire before she was married.

"Remember when we went hunting for coyotes?" Young Alma started the conversation. The whole family started laughing, this was a family classic. Nephi looked over at Claire. "Yea, Claire over there getting us all to kneel in prayer so that we wouldn't get eaten." The whole room echoed with laughter. "Hey, we were safe in the end weren't we." Claire chided back mockingly.

The Thomas family had the sense of humor that would make the circus clowns squirm in their chairs. Funny to them was quite the pain to the ears for anyone not in the loop. When they got going, puns would rain from the ceiling.

As silly as they were, these types of get togethers were cherished by Claire. No matter the differences or pains the family was experiencing, an event like this could heal wounds and bring the family back together.

"Remember when Aunt Pam took Dads keys." Lucy said, not thinking through what she was saying. Pam stiffened up and looked over at Missy. This one was a little too delicate for the family.

The room was swept with awkward silence. Lucy instantly regretted her comment and put her head down. Trying help poor Lucy, Missy chimed in. "If you thought taking the keys was funny. You should have seen when Aunt Pam put the whole wad of Dad's gum in her mouth." Missy had eased the tension. "I almost choked to death." Pam replied. The room burst into tears with laughter.

The kids loved it when the moms got going. They would always Hollywood the best shocked faces and then steamroll the kids with drop the mike comebacks.

Not finished with the first story, Alma brought the family back to the coyote hunting. "The funniest thing of that day was poor Brother Melvin." Alma said. Pausing while all the kids burst again remembering the situation. "Don't go there." Claire said laughing. "I thought he was going to kill Nephi." Nephi took the cue. "Claire, you are a dead eye. I swear you saved my life."

Everyone was laughing now except for Aunt Jane. She had never forgotten that day either and knew the remainder of the story. She had never gotten over her interaction with Claire. This story was a sore spot for her.

"Hey, my Claire is something isn't she." Missy began. Before Missy could get to the punchline, Jane jumped in. "Enough of this story." Jane said. "You weren't the one that got the tongue lashing." Jane was trying to be serious, but the image was too funny. The family burst into laughter again.

Jane laughed a little remembering the situation. Claire caught Jane's eye and knew why she was uncomfortable.
"Enough of this reminiscing." Claire said, stopping the conversation. I want to discuss the plans for my reception.

The family settled down. "I am expecting everyone to be on their best behavior." Claire said giving an eye at the younger ones. "I don't want any issues before Mom, Dad, and I go to the endowment house."

Jane looked up. "Your mom can't go through the endowment house." Jane said without thinking. She then caught herself and looked over at Missy apologetically. The room fell silent.

"What are you saying?" Claire stammered. Missy dropped her head into the chair beside her. Knowing she could not get out of this Aunt Jane continued. "Your mom took her garments off. They have to be placed back on her before she can enter." No words needed to be spoken. In an instant the room had been cleared.

The laughter that filled the ether was now tension-filled angst. Anger started welling up in Claire. "What are you doing Aunt Jane? Why are you torturing Mom?" I didn't mean to." Jane said. "I'm sorry it slipped. Your mom was going to tell you." Jane looked over at Missy again, who had her head down. "Like this!" Claire's anger was at a peak.

"Calm down Claire." Missy said. "I should have told you sooner." Missy looked over to Jane. "It's okay Jane,"

Missy said. "This is my fault." Jane got up and put her hand on Missy's shoulder. "I'll leave you two alone." Jane then walked out of the room.

"Mom?" Claire came and sat down by Missy. "You can't be at my wedding?" Missy leaned against her daughter. "Oh, Claire." Missy started. "You know I took my garments off." Claire knew this but hadn't thought of what the consequences might be. "Mom, not being able to see your daughter married is cruel." Claire said, as she started to cry. "Didn't you notice I didn't go through with Ruth?" Missy asked. "What happens there is so secret Mom." Claire replied. "I had no idea what was going on."

"Mom I need you, please." Claire continued but didn't know how to finish her thoughts. "I love you dear." Missy replied. "Garments are a symbol of the covenants we make in the temple. I think it is ridiculous but taking them off for most people in the group signifies you broke those covenants. That is why they won't let me be there. I am not allowed to enter the temple again until I have my garments placed back on."

Claire looked at her mother. "Why don't you get them placed back on Mom?" Claire asked hoping there might be a solution. Missy lowered her head. "Claire," Missy took a breath. "Do you remember our conversation about the Group and your Dad?" Claire thought for a moment. "Do you mean where you said the Group was at fault for what Dad did to you?" Missy nodded her head.

"What does that have to do with this Mom?" Claire asked. Missy looked up at Claire. "I knew what I was doing when I took my garments off." Missy replied. "At the time they were a symbol of everything wrong with the Group. They felt like chains dragging me under water." Missy wiped a tear from her eye. "They were drowning me Claire."

Claire hesitated, not sure if she wanted to hear her mother's reply, but knew she had to ask her next question. "Mom, do you still feel that way?" "More than ever Claire." Missy started crying. "I shouldn't be telling you this now. You are about to get married. That is why I haven't said anything."

Claire was crying now. "Mom, I need to know. Not having you at my wedding is killing me. Can't you just put your garments back on for me?" Claire said, knowing her comments were selfish.

Missy had stopped crying. Wiping her eyes, she replied to Claire. "Claire, If I put those garments back on the Group has won. They will validate everything your father did." Missy's chest was heaving with adrenaline. "I don't want to ever go back in the endowment house."

"What about me?" Claire said. "I'm so scared. I don't even know what goes on in there. We aren't allowed to know anything." Claire paused for a moment. "Having you there Mom, I know I could do it. Without you." Missy put her hand up to stop Claire.

"Don't you go there Claire." Missy said. "I am fighting my battles. They don't have to be yours." "Do you love

Willie?" Missy asked. Claire looked down. "I think I do, no I do love him Mom." Claire replied. "He is kind and nothing like Ben." Missy kissed her daughter. "Then that is what matters Claire." Missy said. "Just know that I will support you and love you no matter what choices you make." Claire put her arms around her mother and hugged her tightly.

"Now," Missy said. "You need to be happy. You are getting married to a wonderful man. You don't need sadness and anger around you."

Just then Alma walked into the room. Pausing when he saw the expression on the two women's faces, Alma asked, "Sorry, am I interrupting?" "No Dad," Claire replied. "We were just finishing."

....

Elevated from his time alone in the closet a few days earlier and the bonding he and Sallie had afterwards, Willie was now ready to move forward with marrying Claire. He knew now the Lord wanted this marriage. Willie had not shared his feelings with Sallie yet. The two were so focused on the moment in the shed; they had not yet resolved their conflict in words.

Sallie had done some soul searching of her own after the harsh meeting earlier with Willie. As often happens in marriage between a man a woman, messages get entangled in the incompatible design of a mind that is man and woman.

Willie's concerns caused Sallie to be honest with her feelings. She didn't want to hear it from Willie at the time, but when she was alone, Sallie finally admitted to herself she wasn't ready for plural marriage either. As good as Claire was, this might not be the right time.

Sallie wanted to tell this to Willie, but in the moment, she was just glad to be with her husband. She hoped her actions in the barn showed Willie that she was now on his side.

And so is the mis conglobation of the matter. Both Willie and Sallie had shown their acceptance of each other physically. In the midst of coming together, each had unknowingly taken the other's position.

....

It was now the day of the reception. Just hours to go and Sallie had finally gotten up the courage to open her feelings to her husband. Knowing this could not wait any longer, Sallie began. "Willie, about our fight the other day. I know we made up, but I never told you how I felt." "I feel exactly the same," replied Willie. "The moment was too perfect for words." Willie said with a smile. "I agree." Sallie blushed. "Well I think now is the time for words." "Go ahead love," Willie encouraged.

Sallie sat down next to Willie. "I wanted to let you know you are my Priesthood head and I was out of line. I should have followed your direction as the head of the family. After giving it a lot of thought, I realized you were right." Sallie leaned on Willie's shoulder but noticed he had gone stiff.

"What do you mean?" Willie asked. Sallie could see the color leaving Willie's cheeks in the reply. "I, uh, well, this is hard to say, but I don't think we should go through with this marriage. I love Claire and all, but I was fighting my feelings all along. I think you were right." Sallie said this less confidently watching Willie's expression change.

Nothing could prepare Sallie for the next few minutes. In fact, these few minutes drove a rift in this once endeared marriage that never fully healed.

"Willie, what is going on?" Sallie was now frightened by the change in Willie. Willie stood and took a couple steps. He then turned around with a stern look on his face. Sallie had never seen him like this before. Willie had always been so loving. She had dealt with her abusive father her whole life. Sallie knew Willie's stance well. This is the first time in their marriage Willie held this form, a Priesthood man standing in his power.

"Sallie," Willie said with a stern voice. "We are going through with this marriage. I have had a witness that this is what God wants and I will do what he says." Willie was very rigid in his words, emphasizing the finality of what he was saying.

"What, what are you talking about Will?" Sallie changed her tone now sensing the battle about to begin. Sallie tried to soften, hoping Willie would follow suit. "I was so hard on you, as your wife and your helpmeet, I think I went too far. What did I do? What changed?" Sallie was doing everything she could to quell the storm, but it was too late.

Willie had the fire of God. "You are right Sal," Willie took a deep breath. "You are my wife. I make the final decisions in this family."

"How dare you." Sallie screamed at Willie. "You have never treated me like this. Why now?" Willie raised his finger in the air. "Sallie, I received a witness from the Lord. You are being tempted by the devil. I strongly encourage you to go repent before God and cast that spirit out."

This comment shook Sallie into anger. "Oh really," Sallie got right in Willie's face. "Yesterday you came to me in tears looking for a loving understanding wife. Today you demand obedience. I think it is you." "Enough!" Willie cut Sallie off. "I have made my decision. I expect you to support me in this." Sallie fell to her knees in tears. "Willie?" Is all Sallie could say.

Seeing Sallie in tears allowed Willie to regain his composure and soften a little. Willie knelt by Sallie, but she leaned away. "I need you to support me Sal." Willie said.

Sallie's heart was ratcheting through her chest. Seeing her father in Willie was more than she could bear, and she burst into tears of emotion. "Why Willie? I saw you the other day; I know you didn't want this. I try to stand by your side and now you tear me down. You're tearing me apart. What do you want from me? Please Willie."

"We are doing this." Willie said in a monotone voice. "I need you to support me. That is what I want." Sallie got up and ran into her room.

Chapter 16
The Reception

Still recovering from the conversation earlier in the day with her mother, Claire was getting ready for the reception. Taylor had come over to spend time with her friend and help with her hair.

Claire and Taylor had not spent much time together since Claire started dating Willie. Being back with her friend was rejuvenating for Claire. "It's so good to just sit and be with you Taylor, like old times." Claire said as Taylor was doing her hair. "Same here. I've missed you." Taylor replied.

The two caught up on the last few months as Taylor continued doing Claire's hair. Taylor could tell during the conversation Claire was not her normal self. "Claire, something is up." Taylor said. "We're talking but you are on another galaxy. Come on, open up. What's goin on?"

"It's nothing Taylor, you wouldn't understand." Claire responded. "Try me girl." Taylor replied. "I've been around your little band here long enough and heard plenty." Claire looked at Taylor through the mirror. "I don't know Taylor, it's about my mom." Taylor leaned over so she could look directly at Claire. "Is she in trouble again?" Taylor asked.

Claire looked down. "No, well, she can't be at my wedding." The words leaving her mouth brought a tear down Claire's cheek. "Did she do something wrong?" Taylor asked, seeing the emotion from Claire. "No, she broke one of the laws and isn't allowed in to see the marriage." Claire replied.

Taylor stepped back from doing Claire's hair not knowing what to say. Seeing this, Claire continued. "See I told you. You wouldn't understand." Taylor went back to doing Claire's hair. "I'm just trying to process it is all. What law did she violate?" "She took her garments off." Claire replied.

Claire saw the blank stare from Taylor. "You know, the underwear." Claire said. "Oh those," Taylor replied. "That was it. I thought you were going to say she killed someone." Taylor smiled at Claire through the mirror. "Stop it Taylor." Claire said chuckling a little. "It's a big deal." "Okay," Taylor responded. "Why did she take them off?" "It was when my dad married Aunt Pam." Claire said trying not to move her head.

"You polygamists is so weird," Taylor said and jabbed her elbow into Claire's side. "I understand your mom not goin, but me? What have I done to deserve not seeing my best friend gettin hitched." Taylor was trying to lighten things up and ease some of the stress Claire was going through. "Stop it," Claire retorted with a smile. "If this is your idea of helping, it isn't working."

Taylor stopped on Claire's hair and sat down by her. "All kiddin aside Claire, I don't get any of it. From what you've told me in the past, this Group of yours has some strange beliefs." "Don't remind me Taylor." Claire said. "Let me finish," Taylor responded. "If this is the way of the Group, you are going to have to deal with the negative sometimes. I know your mom will be supporting you in her way. I'm not seeing her cryin."

Taylor put her arm around Claire. "You're getting married. That needs to be your focus. Be happy. I know that is what your mom wants. So, let's do it."

Claire was surprised at how understanding Taylor was and how she knew just what to say. "Thank you Taylor." Claire got out of her chair and hugged her best friend. "And we aren't that weird." Claire said jokingly. "Oh yes you are." Taylor replied. They both started laughing.

Taylor went back to doing Claire's hair. Claire then spoke up again. "You may not be able to see me get married, but I expect you to be right there giving me a hug when we come out. Promise?" Claire pled with her eyes through the mirror. Taylor looked back at her. "I hate that compound, but for you, I'll be there." Taylor said winking at Claire. "Now wipe them tears and let me finish your hair. We're goin to be late for your reception."

....

The Group owned property a few miles up the canyon from Pleasant Hills. The property was beloved by the Group. A stream carved through the canyon. Over the eons of time the stream had cleared out a 5-acre meadow, encircling it as the stream wound down the canyon.

The Group had turned this into gorgeous recreational grounds. In the center they had built a large out-door pavilion. The rest of the meadow was filled with a large grassy field surrounded by dozens of camp sites.

The Group as a whole loved to frequent this oasis. Being just a few miles away, this is also where all Pleasant Hills Order receptions were held.

Claire had gone up the canyon with her family. Taylor drove up alone in her new car. New is taking great license as the car was a 10-year-old sedan. Taylor had been working a year to save up the money needed to buy a car. It wasn't pretty, but it was hers and it was her pride and joy.

"Yay, I get to go stand out like a sore thumb all over again." Taylor was thinking to herself I she drove up to the meadow. "Claire's going to be so occupied tonight, I just get to chill with all the polyg kids. So much fun. They just love us gentiles."

Although most of the Order recognized Taylor, she was still an outsider. She was allowed to be there, but no one was too interested to warm her into their presence. Taylor remembered the night she was sent home like it was yesterday. Since that time, she had no interest to get to know anyone else from the Group.

Taylor found a table on the side and sat down to watch the events. This was the first time Claire had been to one of these receptions. She chuckled a little when she saw what looked like a Congo line form in front of Claire.

Taylor watched as Claire, Willie, and Sallie greeted the line. One by one every Order member was walking by and talking for a few seconds. A quick hug and then repeat with the next. "Sheesh, Willie and Sallie sure look happy." Taylor said to herself sarcastically. They would smile as people congratulated them, but Taylor could see they were distant and not in a very good mood. "At least Claire looks happy."

Having nothing better to do and feeling very out of place, Taylor started a game of seeing if she could identify all the wives for each man. She knew a lot of the teenagers as she had grown up around them, but the parents Taylor had rarely seen. "Oh, those two look happy." Taylor said to herself seeing two women next to each other. "Nope." Taylor said again and watched as two men came and sat between the two women.

It didn't take long for Taylor to master her new game. The ones not liking each other tended to be the ones with the same man. "Ooh, that one shut down right when the other came over. Cha Ching, right again."

After playing this game for a while, Taylor started looking more and more over at Claire. It was subconscious at first, but then she started to wonder. "Is this what Claire is getting into?" Taylor knew of the Group and their polygamy, but she had never really seen the Group in action.

She had been over to Claire's house many times, but it was usually just to hang out. Taylor had only seen Claire's dad a few times in all the years she knew Claire. He did not seem to be around much.

She avoided Jane and knew the sad tale of Pam coming into the family, but Taylor had never really made any connections to the culture and how the beliefs were infecting people's lives.

"I have had about enough of this." Taylor said to herself starting to get disgusted. Taylor decided she would wait out the rest of the night in her pride and joy. She wanted to leave desperately but had promised Claire she would stay help with the cleanup.

"It is now just you and me baby." Taylor rolled down the window to feel the mountain coolness of the summer evening. Taylor had the seat all the way back resting her eyes when she was startled by speaking around the corner.

Anticipating others wanting to leave before her, Taylor had parked her car on the side of the pavilion. Around the corner on the back side of the pavilion Taylor could hear two men in conversation.

Taylor recognized Willie's voice. "I just had to get away for a few minutes." Willie said. "Sallie and I had it out this morning and now she won't even look at me. "Women," the other voice said in a sarcastic tone. "What ticks me off," Willie continued, "is she was the one wanting me to do this. And then I get an answer from God, and she completely flips." "Say no more friend." The other voice said. "If they aint nagging you for something they are tearing into you for God knows what. Can't win no matter what."

There was a pause in the conversation. Then Willie spoke up again. "I'm doing this for her Ben. I don't do this and what, we be servants in the celestial kingdom at best?" Willie raised his voice. "I'd get kicked out of the order if I didn't marry Claire now."

Taylor then heard Ben reply. "Willie, stay the course bro. She'll come around. I've seen Claire, she'll be a good second wife for Sallie, very obedient." "Yeah I know, Claire is perfect. She'll be an easy wife to deal with."

"So, you do love her?" Ben said with a clear jesting tone. "You were right bro." Willie responded. "It isn't about love. It's what God wants."

"Dude, you gonna get the goods tomorrow night. Am I right?" Taylor could hear the two laughing. "Shut up man." Willie said. "Once again you are such a prick. Can't say I haven't thought of it though." Taylor could hear the two burst into laughter as they walked away.

Fearing to be discovered, Taylor laid frozen during the whole exchange. She almost lost it when Willie said he didn't love Claire. It was even more when the two started joking about the wedding night.

"That ass hole," Taylor uttered in disgust. "She is no object to be won. These damn polygamists commit adultery right in front of their wives, and they are using my Claire to do it. Ooh, that ass hole."

Taylor was steaming. "If I catch him alone, I'd slap his ass so hard." There was still thirty minutes to go before the reception was over. Taylor could not stay seated. She got out of her car and started walking down the canyon road trying to cool off before she saw Claire again.

....

With so many people interacting with her left and right, Claire was oblivious to any misgivings between Willie and Sallie. She did notice Willie leave abruptly for a few minutes and saw Sallie walk the other way, but Claire didn't think much of it.

Claire had always loved the Group receptions. This one being hers, the reception was tiring for Claire, but she didn't mind. Regardless of what was happening between Willie and Sallie, Claire was enjoying herself.

From a distance someone like Taylor could see the bigger picture, but Willie was always careful to show his best face when interacting with Claire. Willie was still in that genetically male dating mode charming his image into perfection.

Claire had given no thought to Taylor during the reception. Claire knew Taylor would be somewhat uncomfortable, so it was no surprise she had not seen Taylor for a while. The reception was now coming to an end there were only a few people remaining. Claire was a little surprised when she didn't see Taylor anywhere.

Willie and Sallie had already left. It was an unspoken expectation in the Group that the man and his first wife would leave early from the reception. No one raised an eyebrow when Claire was there alone. That is no one except Taylor. Coming back up the road after seeing several cars pass by, Taylor knew the reception was coming to an end.

After calming down on her walk, Taylor decided it was probably best to not say anything to Claire. She was pretty sure Claire would not be happy with her. Seeing Claire, Taylor went to talk with her. Taylor was relieved to not see Willie around.

Claire looked at Taylor as she approached. "Where have you been? I was looking everywhere." "Oh, I just went for a walk." Taylor replied. Claire smiled. "Hopefully it was not too weird."

"Where's Willie?" Taylor asked, changing the subject. "Oh, he left early with Sallie." Claire replied. "Figures," Taylor said under her breath. "What was that?" Claire asked. "Oh nothing." Taylor responded. "Let's go clean up."

Avoiding any further conversation with Claire, Taylor went to cleaning up around the pavilion. Once done, Taylor headed to her car. "Wait for me silly." Claire shouted to Taylor as she was walking away. Taylor had forgotten they had agreed to ride back together.

After giving her family a hug, Claire got into the car with Taylor. "You are sure in a hurry to leave." Claire said. "Was it that bad?" Claire was thinking Taylor was feeling out of place, and this was the reason for her actions.

"No, the reception was fine." Taylor said. "You looked so beautiful up there." "Why thank you." Claire smiled. "I can't believe I am getting married. Thank you so much for helping me get my head straight." Claire leaned over and gave her friend a kiss on the cheek. Taylor gave Claire a smile, and they headed down the canyon.

Driving down the road, Taylor was full of mixed feelings. Her best friend was happier than she had seen in a while. It was killing her to know the joy was not shared by Willie. Taylor was scared for what Claire was getting into. Seeing the Group, and more specifically, Willie a lot clearer, Taylor had a knot in her stomach for what she dreamed was the future for her friend.

Wanting to start a conversation with her friend on her last night of being single, Claire looked over at Taylor. "What do you think of Willie? Isn't he so cute?" "Hmm." This was the only sound Taylor could utter in reply. "That is all you can say." Claire laughed at her friend. "Come on speak to me. This is our last night being single together."

Taylor kept her eyes on the road. "I guess I am not in a talking mood Claire." "You?" Claire laughed again. "No way, please I need one last girl talk like old times." Claire, being so young, had that sense of finality when big events happen. Her youthfulness did not let her see life moving as normal beyond major events.

This talk, innocent as it was, was the worst thing for Taylor to hear. The prying from Claire was tearing into Taylor's resolve. As Claire kept pushing, Taylor broke.

Not able to contain herself, Taylor let her words slip out.

"He doesn't love you Claire." Taylor said, with a burst of emotion, regretting what she said as soon as it was in the open. "What are you saying?" Claire said in an instant change of expression. Taylor looked away. "Sorry, I don't know what I was saying. Let's just get home."

"Taylor, stop this car now." Claire said. "I am not letting you off that easy." As Taylor pulled over, Claire continued. "What a mean thing to say Taylor. Where did that come from?" Claire was visibly upset.

Taylor pulled off the road and looked forward, not daring to meet the gaze that was focused her. Trying to understand the sudden outburst, Claire spoke again. "Taylor, I don't understand this. I know we are different. Is this what you are trying to do, convince me to do what the world wants me to do? I thought we agreed not to push each other."

Taylor had no clue where to go from here. She just sat there looking forward. "Are you going to say anything?" Claire said. "You have been so much to me. Why wait until the night before my wedding?"

"It's not that," Taylor started. She knew not saying anything was making it worse. Claire kept the gaze waiting for her friend to continue. Taylor spoke up again. "Claire, I meant not to say anything. You just kept asking."

"What are you saying?" Claire asked trying to read what her friend was saying. Taylor finally looked over at Claire. "I heard him speaking to his friend. He is only doing this for Sallie. He doesn't love you he is just doing this out of duty." Taylor paused for a moment. "Claire, I heard him speak of you like you were nothing. I don't want you to be hurt. Claire I am so sorry. I wasn't going to say anything." The last words Taylor said in tears as she saw her friend's face.

"I am hurt Taylor." Claire responded after a few moments of silence. "My best friend, turning on me the night before my wedding. Please take me home." "Claire?" Taylor pleaded. "Sorry Taylor," Claire replied a tear in her eye now. "I just want to go home."

Taylor drove Claire the rest of the way. The two did not say anything else to each other.

Chapter 17
The Endowment

Fifty miles north of Pleasant Hills is the town of Scottsdale. A small range of hills lies just beyond the town. As the hill is crests, the land drops into a bowl made of mountains surrounding the entire area. On the east rim of the bowl lies an inconspicuous road. This road winds down into the bowl where it terminates at a gawdy parking lot.

In the center of the parking lot is a group of three buildings. The REC is on the side. A homestead is just beyond. Flanking the REC is a house, where at first glance does not look like anything extra ordinary. A second glance reveals this house is more well-kept than the other buildings. This house is the endowment house.

An endowment house serves the same purpose as a temple. The Group shies away from building temples as one day they believe the church's temple doors will be open to the Group. Temples stand above endowment houses in that they have a Holy of Holies, which is a sacred room believed to be an earthly residence of God. In ancient times in Solomon's temple, the Holy of Holies is where the ark of the covenant sat.

Without a Holy of Holies, a temple, well, is not a temple. The Group only considers a few of the church's temples as true temples because the church rarely adds the Holy of Holies room these days. The pinnacle of all temples is the Salt Lake temple. This is the direction all Group members face when praying.

The purpose of endowment houses and temples is sealing people together for eternity. More specifically, this is where marriages are performed.

The Group's endowment house has a front door, but that is not where its secrets lie. The front door only leads to offices. The true magic comes in the form of a seemingly meaningless door next to a garage on the side of the house. Enter this door and you have entered the Lord's house.

Look to the left and you will see dressing rooms. Look to right and you will see additional rooms that almost look like showers. Straight ahead is a baptismal font shimmering in the distance, as baptismal fonts are always on the basement level. This is where baptisms for the dead occur. The baptisms serve another purpose for the Group and are not part of the endowment ceremony.

The showers mentioned before are where the endowment story begins. Within these shower rooms a ritual bath is given to a person. There is no water used in the bath. It is all done with oils consecrated for this purpose.

The bath is administered with five points of a person's body being touched. These points are the forehead, nipples, belly, genitals, and knee. This part of the endowment alone has caused a lot of hurt in the Group. As the Group is not allowed to speak of what happens to those not endowed, a lot of newly initiated members are caught off guard. In some cases, people administering the ceremony have gone to the point of groping the person receiving the endowment. Though not spoken openly, many Group members carry scars from this event.

After this washing and anointing, the person is then given a new name. This name is determined beforehand and is typically a name from the Bible or Book of Mormon. All members going through on that day receive the same name. Each person is instructed to never repeat out loud or tell anyone else this name. That at least applies to the men. The women tell one person, their husband, which comes later in the endowment. The man is after all a god to his wife. He knows her new name. She is to never know his.

At this point, the garments are placed on the person, who is told the garments are never to be removed again and will act as a protection to the person for the remainder of their life.

After the garments are placed on the person they then dress in white clothing. They are then led to the Telestial room. The telestial room is on the basement floor and is finely decorated to represent the garden of Eden. The room symbolizes the lowest level of heaven.

In this room the person takes their first covenant and utters a penalty oath swearing to never reveal what happens in the temple. They seal this oath with a death gesture saying they would rather die than break this oath.

From there, the person ascends a flight of stairs to the Terrestrial room. This room is nice but is not too memorable. A similar pattern occurs at the Telestial room where the person takes another covenant and swears another penalty oath.

Stairs are ascended once again, this time terminating at a curtain with holes in it. The curtain symbolizes the veil into heaven.

At the veil, a person is given secret signs that are used as keys to enter heaven. The signs are then done through the holes in the curtain. For the men, the person on the other side is said to be God. The man gives his new name to this person and does the signs. He is then allowed to pass through the veil.

A woman does all the same, but on the other side of the veil her husband stands rather than god. For the Group, a woman is introduced to god through their husband. He, in essence, stands in the place of god for his family.

Prior to the veil, the men and women are kept on opposite sides of the room. Once they pass through the veil, the remainder of the ceremony is done with the couple together.

If a woman is a plural wife, her husband to be will enter the ceremony at this point as he is already endowed. This will be the first time the two see each other during the ceremony.

The couple then Pass through the veil and are led into an elaborately decorated room. This is the celestial room, the pinnacle of the endowment. The final covenants and oaths are given in this room.

Beyond this room are sealing rooms, which are used for marriage ceremonies. For the Group, marriage is part of the endowment where men and women are sealed together for eternity.

These sealing rooms each have an alter in the center with mirrors at each end so that the couple can see multiple reflections of each other, which represents eternity.

The couple then kneel at the alter across from each other. If it is a plural marriage, the first wife offers the new wife to kneel at the altar. The couple are then married in a somewhat catholic fashion where they each vow to each other and God for eternity. The couple then kiss across the alter for the first time as man and wife.

In addition to the oaths and covenants taken during the endowment, the person also has additional clothing added to them as they ascend through the ceremony.

By the time they get to the end, the garb is an array of different articles of cloth, with men and women dressed in white with a green apron spread across their mid-section.

The only temple clothing a person takes with them outside the endowment house is their garments, which are seen as a symbol of everything that happened during the ceremony.

This is the endowment ceremony. This is how marriage is performed within the group. The endowment is so sacred to members of the Group that they are not allowed to speak of it. Learning the endowment is a trial by fire of sorts. The person receiving the endowment for the first time learns it as they go.

Chapter 18
Marriage

Claire tossed all night. "I feel sick," she mumbled as she leaned over to Missy in bed. It was a Group tradition where the mom would sleep with daughter the night before the wedding to provide comfort and reassurance.

"That is a common reaction," Missy chuckled. "I remember I had a fever of 102 my wedding day. By the time the ceremony was over I could barely remember I was sick."

"That helps," Claire mumbled again, not wanting to continue the conversation. Missy's words of reassurance were comforting but had missed the mark. Claire had been tossing all night thinking of her conversation with Taylor the night before.

Taylor's outburst bounced from ear to ear refusing to give her any relief. "What a way to start a wedding day." Claire thought to herself. "Why did Taylor have to run her mouth like that? I thought we agreed to respect each other's beliefs. Why is she meddling and ruining my relationship with Willie? I know this is the right thing to do. God wants me to marry Willie." Claire was going over all her interactions, convincing herself this was the right thing to do.

"Taylor doesn't just make things up." Claire thought again to herself. That is what was troubling her so much. "I will pull Willie to the side before the endowment starts." Claire thought to herself as she came up with a plan of reassurance. "I'm sure he will clarify what Taylor had overheard."

Claire was in the middle of her pep talk when Missy reached over and gave her a hug. Seeing a tear in Claire's eye Missy said, "It will be ok dear. Today you get to be married. I know you are nervous, but it will all end well. You will see."

Claire burst into tears. "I cannot do this without you Mom. Why can't you be there?" Missy held Claire tighter, mustering the inner strength all mothers have, the strength to cover your pain when your child is in need.

"In time dear, this will be a distant memory." Missy said. "Just know, I will be outside praying for you with all my heart." "Mom," the only word Claire could whisper but a word made for this moment. "I know, I know." A tear down Missy's cheek, the two held each other in silence.

....

The endowment is an all-day event. For the Pleasant Hills Order, it was even longer as they had an hour drive to Scottsdale.

The sun was not yet up when the Thomas family arrived at the endowment house. Bishop Korban was waiting at the door and checked the recommends of Claire, Dad, Aunt Jane, and aunt Pam. Knowing the situation, he didn't check Missy's recommend.

Claire looked around for Willie and Sallie's car, but they had not yet arrived. "Are you ready for the great day?" Bishop Korban asked. "I am," Claire replied in a nervous voice.

Endowment proceedings were sacred and only discussed in the building. It is considered inappropriate to study the endowment or learn about what happens there prior to being endowed. Claire had a little bit of an idea of what was going to happen but was mainly in the dark. She had been preparing for this day her whole life, but the suddenness and not knowing what was going to happen had Claire shaking a little.

This adding to her words with Taylor was making Claire more and more jittery. "Where is Willie?" Claire said, leaning over to Aunt Jane. "Don't worry dear." she replied. "Won't I see him before we start? When will be the next time I see him?"

"Hush now dear," Missy leaned in. "I will be in the front lawn when you come out." "Mom," Claire uttered, but she was moved inside by her father before she could finish. "It's time dear." Alma said. "let's go in." Missy was left at the door, not able to have final words with her daughter.

....

Imagine the feeling of walking into a haunted house. There is unknown around every corner, well that is somewhat the feeling Claire had walking into the endowment house.

Now that Claire was inside the endowment house, she was trying to forget everything else and focus on the moment. For some reason, the building felt creepy to her. "The peak of God's commandments, why am I so fearful?" Claire thought to herself. "Feel the spirit. God is with me."

Claire knew about the temple clothing and the garments. She had seen her mom's garments many times and grew up with the stories of their protection. Sister Bransen had given her the bag of temple cloths two days earlier with the strict instruction to not look at them.

"I wonder when I put these on." Claire thought to herself. She was trying to imagine and anticipate everything that was going to happen. "Stop shaking dear." said Aunt Jane, when she saw Claire. "I'll be with you the whole time." Claire smiled at Jane grateful for her reassurance.

"Men go on that side and women over here." Jane said. They then entered what looked like a dressing room in a shopping store to Claire. "What do I do Aunt Jane?" Claire asked. "In your bag you will find a white sheet like you see in the hospital. Take all your clothes off and put the sheet on." Jane responded. "Let me know when you are ready, and I will come and get you when they are ready."

"All of my clothes?" Claire leaned in and whispered to Aunt Jane nervously. "Yes dear." Jane replied "You are about to be washed and anointed. This will clean your body in preparation of receiving the garments." "Oh, ok," Claire responded. That didn't sound too bad to Claire. It made sense, but what was odd to Claire was she didn't remember seeing any shower stalls or tubs.

"I am ready Aunt Jane." Claire said. "Ok dear." Jane replied. "Give us a few minutes." After a moment, Jane spoke again through the curtain. "Claire, in your bag you will see garments. Do you know what they look like?" "Yes I do." Claire replied. "Good," Jane said. "Pull them out and take care nothing in the bag touches the floor."

A few minutes later Aunt Jane pulled the curtain open. "Come with me." Seeing Claire's white face, Jane smiled. "This is so exciting." Aunt Jane said trying to make Claire feel better.

Garments in hand, and feeling very exposed in the small gown with no sides, Claire walked into an adjacent stall, which was about double the size of the one she was in. Stunned, Claire was met by two women, sister Bransen and a woman Claire did not know. All were dressed in white.

"What is this?" Claire asked. "Where are the showers?" The three sisters chuckled to each other. "Stand here Sister Claire," said Sister Bransen. "Washings and anointings are done with oils."

The unknown woman then started reciting what sounded like a ritual chant and then wiped oil on Claire's forehead. She then said a few more words and then put her hands underneath Claire's robe. Claire grabbed the woman's hand. "What are you doing?"

Claire asked. Claire had always been a private person, being the girl who dressed in the corner in public restrooms. Even among women, she did not like being seen.

The woman got flustered and looked over at Jane. "It will be alright dear." Jane said. "Now put your hands down and no more speaking." Claire froze as the elderly sister reached under the robe and touched her body. She almost screamed when she was touched in unexpected places. A tear came to her eye as the woman kept going lower.

At this point the rest of the endowment would be a blur to Claire. Later in life Claire could only recall one or two points mentioned in the endowment ceremony. This was a house where God resided. She was not ready for this. "Why did God see the need to have people feel all over her body?"

Claire tried to hide the tear as the sisters then began walking her into her new garments. "Isn't this so spiritual?" One of the sisters spoke softly when she saw Claire's tear.

Claire wanted to leave, but she was stuck. Knowing nothing else to do, Claire swallowed and kept going.

The next thing Claire could remember was she was in her temple dress sitting in a room with a fake tree on the wall and a slightly lighter temple bag in hand. She was on one side with the women. The men were on the other side. Several people she recognized in the group, but Claire was surprised by how many faces she did not recognize. Willie was not there.

Aunt Jane sat down by Claire. "I will help give you assistance through the rest of the ceremony Claire." Jane said. "Pay attention and I will tell you what to do."

After everyone was seated, Brother Levi stood up and started speaking. "Why is he so angry?" Claire thought to herself. Everyone stood up. Then all of the sudden Brother Levi made a slitting motion across his neck. The actual words spoken were different from what Claire remembered. All she heard was, "I would die if I revealed anything that happened here."

The members were then asked to stand and repeat the gesture. "I can't Aunt Jane." Claire whispered trying to not bring attention to herself. Aunt Jane no longer had a smile on her face. Jane didn't need to say anything. Claire could tell she could not get out of this.

"Darn Willie." Claire thought to herself. "Making me go through this alone." Claire was starting to feel the walls collapse around her. She was trapped and knew she could not go anywhere.

Two more unwanted death threat gestures later and a couple more rooms, and Claire found herself dressed in a robe bonnet, green apron, and moccasins. Had everyone not been dressed the same, Claire would have died with embarrassment for how she was dressed.

Tears had become a little more frequent, but her feelings were easily overlooked by others in this setting.

Thankfully, Aunt Jane had come prepared and kept Claire supplied with tissues.

"Claire, you are next." Aunt Jane whispered. Not really getting what was going on, Claire walked up to a curtain with holes in it. One of the holes opened. "Willie!" Claire blurted. "Shush," Willie motioned to her with a stern face. Claire didn't mind. At least he was there. Willie stopped speaking and was staring at Claire. Confused, she looked at Aunt Jane. "Martha," Aunt Jane whispered. Claire had totally forgotten the name she was given.

"Martha." Claire said. Willie then embraced her through the curtain, which took Claire by surprise. It was the first time the two had hugged, curtain in between or otherwise. Willie then put his arm out and led Claire through the curtain.

....

Taylor had been at the group compound once before with Claire. Claire's brother Nephi was playing basketball in the REC building next to the endowment house. This time, however, was different.

As Taylor came down the hill a huge sense of trepidation fell over her. Taylor was hurt by Claire's parting words the day before, but something drew her there. Regardless of her hate for the situation, Claire was her friend. Taylor thought if she saw Claire it would make amends somehow. "I am still convinced Willie does not love her, but I went too far." Taylor said to herself. "Claire is my best friend."

Pulling into the large parking lot, Taylor started getting a high level of anxiety. "This was a mistake." Taylor said to herself. "What will the Group people do if they see me here? Am I allowed to be here?" Feeling very uneasy, Taylor parked in the far end of the parking lot from the buildings, right at the entryway.

....

Willie held Claire's hand as they walked into a very beautiful large room. All furnishings were in white. Claire tried to get Willie's attention to let him know she was relieved he was there. Willie gave her a stern look when he saw her expression. Claire tried to say something, but Willie stopped her. "There is no talking in this room." Willie whispered. Claire felt disheveled. "Isn't Willie glad to see me?" Claire thought to herself.

Claire and Willie sat side by side. From another door, Sallie came into the room. Out of habit being married to Willie, Sallie attempted to sit down between the two. Willie motioned to the chair next to Claire. A little embarrassed, Sallie sat down.

Claire looked over to Sallie trying to say hello. Sallie did not return the glance. Claire could see Sallie had been crying. Claire put her hand on Sallie's to comfort her. Sallie gently pulled her hand away and covered her face. "Does no one want me here?" Claire thought to herself. "Why is no one happy?"

All women were then told to veil their faces. "Sallie is crying, can she even breath with that thing on?" Claire thought. She then leaned over to Willie. "Sallie is not looking well. Does she need to cover her face?" "Quiet," Willie motioned with his finger.

The room formed a circle and repeated the oath motions that Claire had done earlier. This sent a shiver down her spine. The circled group then repeated the prayer offered by Brother Jacobs kneeling in the center.

Claire was feeling more exhausted than ever after three long prayers had been offered. "When would this be over?" When will we be married?" Claire thought. Claire started wondering if they were now married. She had never said anything. "Is this how marriages are done?" Claire's heart sank even lower. "Did I miss it?" A deep knot bounced around her stomach. "Oh no, what I have I done."

Willie pulled Claire out of her thoughts. "Claire it is time." Willie looked at Sallie. Sallie reached over and grabbed Claire's hand. "Follow me," Sallie said. Claire took Sallie's hand. Sallie still did not look Claire in the eye and led Claire into a side room with mirrors and an alter in the center.

The room was filled with Claire's family. Dad and Pam were there. Ruth was there sitting along with Wendy and Ben. "Ugh" Claire said inwardly. Jane went and sat down beside Alma and Pam.

Sallie motioned to one side of the alter. "Kneel there," Sallie pointed. Claire now was understanding what the room was for. This is where they would get married. "Mom," Claire accidentally let this word slip out. Aunt

Pam came over and gave Claire a reassuring rub on the shoulder. Claire then looked up across the alter.

Willie was not smiling. He looked just as sick as she was feeling. Claire knelt across from Willie for what seemed like an eternity, probing for any sign of support. Willie just looked past Claire at his reflection in the mirrors. "Was Taylor right? Does he not love me?"

Brother Levi started speaking. Claire's mind started racing. "I want my mom. I am stuck. Is the room collapsing?" Claire's heart started ratcheting in her chest. "This is sick. I hate this place. He doesn't love me. Oh, what is Sallie thinking, what have I done?"

"Sister Claire?" Brother Levi tapped on Claire's shoulder. "What?" Claire said, looking up. "Will you or won't you marry Brother Willie Allen?" Brother Levi replied. "No, no, no, no," Claire's heart screamed inside. Given the world around her there were only two words allowed in this moment. "I will" were the words that left Claire's mouth.

Claire suddenly seemed as she saw the darkness screaming for joy in the mirror in front of her as she looked at a million self-reflections fading into eternity. Her face, the darkness, Claire was now Willie's. It was over.

....

Eight hours walking around the endowment house grounds alone had given Missy a lot of time to think. She was not happy how Alma pulled Claire away without a goodbye. "I saw your glance." Missy said to herself bitterly.

The old thoughts of losing her kids, not knowing what to do, the struggles when she left all came creeping back. Resigned to her station in life, Missy spoke to herself. "It is all for the good. God will provide."

As Missy was pacing in the yard, she saw a car crest the hills and enter into the bowl. "Who is that coming down the hill?" Missy thought to herself.

Missy watched as Taylor drove into the parking lot and sat for a while before finally resting next to the entry. "Oh sweet." Missy thought to herself. "Just like Taylor, always there for her friend."

Missy had grown to love Taylor. She had been through so much with Claire that Missy thought of Taylor as one of her own. Missy could tell by where she was parked, Taylor was trying to not be noticed. "Come on Missy," She said to herself. "The poor girl is probably scared. Let's go over and talk with her."

Missy had gotten just behind Taylor's car when she heard something on the side of the endowment house. "What is going on?" Missy turned in a fright.

....

"The two of you may now kiss." Brother Levi said. Pausing, Willie looked over at Sallie. Claire could see he was searching for approval. Following Willie's eye, Claire caught Sallie's gaze. There were three people not smiling in the room. They were the ones about to spend eternity with each other.

The cherished delay could no longer hold its weight. Willie leaned in for a kiss. "He doesn't love me. She hates me. I hate this place. Mom. Dad, how could you do this to her? Taylor was right." In one leaning instant, reality washed over Claire. The rest of her life was staring at her with endless faces.

"I CAN'T DO THIS!" Claire screamed. The darkness lost its grip. The stunning sound sent a chilling freeze across the room. This freeze was just long enough for adrenaline to pump strength into Claire's legs, and she ran out of the room before the crowd could lasso her back into their embrace.

Violating every sacred room in the haunted house, Claire rushed down the stairs. When she got to the ground floor she burst into the hallway and almost went right into the baptismal font. Catching her balance, Claire looked up. Life was a meaningless looking door next to a garage, and it was now a mere feet away.

"Do not violate this place. Do not shame the family." Alma's words were echoing down the stairs.

....

Taylor was fidgeting with her purse when something caught her eye coming out of the building across the parking lot. Looking up, Taylor's heart exploded as she let out a blood curling scream. "They're coming to kill me."

A ghostly figure came rushing out the side of the white-accented building. Turning on the ignition as fast a she could Taylor lifted her foot to smash the gas pedal. "Aaaahhh!" Taylor let out another blood curling scream and slammed on the brake when she looked up and saw a woman leaning on her hood.

"Take her!" The voice commanded. Regaining a little, Taylor looked again at the mummified white and green figure coming her way. Recognizing the figure, "Claire!" Taylor screamed again.

Some say when fear comes it is narrow and without texture. Taylor learned in this instant that fear has many faces. All of which had flooded her system in a matter of seconds.

Looking back forward she recognized Mrs. Thomas who was now ushering to Claire. "Run!" Missy said, calling to her daughter.

With every last bit of energy, Claire ran towards the car. "Mom, Mom, Mom." Claire panted through heavy tears. The only safe place in the world, Claire fell into her mother's arms. "I couldn't do it Mom. I couldn't." "Mom," that word again, weight of the world in three letters.

In a mother's moment, Missy was now doing for her daughter what she could not do for herself. Sacrificing everything, Missy put her hands on Claire's shoulders. "Claire, I love you, get in that car." Missy demanded.

"Mom?" Claire questioned in tears. Missy looked into Claire's eyes. "If you love me at all, get into that car." Missy could see Alma shortening the distance towards them.

Taylor kicked open the passenger door. "Please Claire, get in. They're coming." Missy hugged Claire and kissed her. A loving kiss, which may be the last touch the two would ever have, mom and daughter separated.

Taylor slammed on the gas pedal, almost crashing the car rounding the corner out of the parking lot. Feeling like Lot's wife turning to a pillar of salt, Claire turned to see her mother fall to her knees and her dad leaning on his legs just beyond.

Claire turned back around and saw Taylor's hand reaching towards her. Claire grasped it tightly. Up the road the friends went, holding hands in tears. A gentile knight, a virago in white, two young heroines rode off. The Group disappeared over the hill, fading in the distance.

Made in the USA
Columbia, SC
03 March 2021

33815819R00120